# THE SECRET 6:
# THE GOLDEN ALLIGATOR

# THE GOLDEN
# ALLIGATOR

*By Robert J. Hogan*

STEEGER BOOKS • 2020

# CHAPTER 1
## BURIED ALIVE

IT WAS midnight. Along the north shore of a Long Island highway a car sped at sixty miles an hour. It was the light sedan of the Secret 6, and its only occupant was King, the leader of that little group of crime breakers whose name had in the past few months, become notorious among the police and the lawless alike.

King raised a hand from the wheel and slapped his face twice to keep from falling asleep. Thank the Lord it wouldn't be long until he'd be back in the snug cabin that the secret band called their jungle home.

His head nodded a little again. For a split second sleep overtook him. The car swerved gently to the side of the road. Tires crunched on the gravel.

The sound caused him to snap wide awake, but he was too late. The car had already struck something. *Bang!* There was a loud report as the air left his right front tire.

King jammed on the brakes—not too hard, so that he wouldn't be thrown farther into the ditch.

*Wham! Crash!* His headlights had shown him a culvert at the side of the road. He had tried to avoid it too late. He felt the whole right front corner of the car crumbling as it struck.

The axle and wheel were folding back. The car was plowing down into the ditch. It stopped with a final jolt that threw him against the wheel, but without injury. With a groan of anger he opened the door and climbed out.

"Well, fella," he said after he had inspected the damage, "it looks as if it's your turn to walk. This would happen right here in the loneliest spot of the whole road."

He pitched over backward with a choking sound.

He stood up and surveyed the whole situation. The more he thought about it, the stranger it seemed that a tire should blow out, because both of them were new.

He walked around to the side of the car, reached into the pocket and took out a flashlight. Then he went back to the right front corner.

The wheel was torn off and crumpled and had been pushed back under the side of the car. He fished it out, found the tire was badly mashed where it had hit the culvert. He shook his head.

"That tire hit something else," he decided half aloud. "I'm sure of it. Yes—here it is. Say, that's a nasty looking hole! Just as though somebody had socked it with an axe."

He walked back fifty feet to the point where he had swerved and looked for the object that had gashed his tire.

He searched perhaps two minutes. Then the beam of his flashlight glinted on something shiny. Stooping down, he picked it up—a pickaxe.

Curious, he swung the light so that it covered the side of the road, but there were no other instruments in sight. Maybe it had dropped off a truck.

Suddenly he tensed. A sound had disturbed the night stillness—a queer sound. It reminded him of the noise that beavers make when they are cutting down trees for a dam. Even as he listened it stopped, then started again. Softly muffled yet rasping, it gave him an eerie feeling that he vainly tried to shake off.

He strode several steps in the direction from which it came, but when he flashed his light the sound ceased abruptly.

He turned off the flash and in the darkness surveyed the territory from which the noise came.

It was merely a field of an abandoned farm and weeds and grass grew in wild disarray. Here and there was a low bush.

Yes, the noise must come from an animal, because there was nothing tall or thick enough to hide a full-grown human being. One minute. Two minutes passed. Then the sound began again.

*Rasp—rasp—rasp!*

King slipped his right hand into his pocket and felt for his gun. Then he remembered he didn't have it with him!

*Rasp—rasp—rasp!*

He mumbled a thought that came into his head.

"If it were three o'clock in the morning and I were in a town I'd swear that it was a second-story man trying to saw his way into a house so quietly that nobody could hear him.

*Rasp—rasp—rasp!*

King advanced now on tiptoe without the aid of his light. Step by step. The noise was slightly louder. No, it was no animal gnawing at something. It held a crisper note. Exactly like someone using a fine saw on wood, but he couldn't locate the direction from which it came.

At one moment he thought it came from directly under him. Then again it seemed to come from farther beyond. He tiptoed on, picking his way gingerly. The sound seemed to come from all about him now, but he didn't dare turn on his light for fear it would stop. And yet he had the most unpleasant feeling that whatever was making the sound might leap out at him at any second. He began to have the sensation of listening to some

5

invisible thing. A ghost, for instance, that made sound but could not be seen.

*Rasp—rasp—rasp!*

He found himself tiptoeing about in a circle. It came from right around there somewhere. Suddenly his foot struck soft earth and his toes sunk in. He put one foot forward to take another step. But the soft earth rose in a pile. He stumbled and fell on his hands and knees.

His out-stretched hand touched something metallic—something like a large pipe. Instantly the rasping sound stopped!

He scrambled to his feet, flashed on his pocket torch. Then he was staring down at what he saw in the light rays.

He had stumbled upon a mound of earth. Out of one end of it extended a stove pipe about six inches in diameter. Perhaps it was a dugout, although there were no other visible openings above the ground.

Tipping his light so that the beam shot down the pipe he stared after it and the sight that met his eyes almost caused him to shudder.

A face was looking up. Blinking at him from the bottom of the stovepipe!

IT WAS not an unpleasant face, but there was desperation and fear written in the expression of the eyes. The lips moved. The man spoke in a voice that was so rasping and strained that it was scarcely audible.

"I tell you I don't know where it's hidden," he said.

"Hey, wait a minute," King shouted. "What is all this?"

Then the parched, strained voice said:

"You ought to know if you're the one that buried me."

"I'm not," King answered.

There was a strange note in his voice as he said it, and at the same time he began digging furiously with his bare hands. He could tell by the length of the stovepipe that the casket was not buried very deeply. There was perhaps a foot of earth above it. And as he worked he talked down.

"Hold on. I'm going to get you out of here. Who was the devil that buried you, anyway?"

"Who are you?" the man in the casket countered.

"That doesn't matter just now," King said. "Just consider me a friend for the time being."

By now he had dug down so that his hands were scraping the top of the casket. The soil was loose, but there were stones there and it gave evidence of having been hard before it was dug up.

"That explains the pickaxe," he thought. "The men who buried this fellow must have been startled, or for some other reason forgot to take the pick along."

A voice reached him through the stovepipe that was the vent in the casket.

"How'd you know I was here?"

"I didn't," said King, "until I heard you trying to saw your way out—or was that what you were trying to do?"

"Yes," said the other. "But I didn't think anyone would hear me. I have been yelling my lungs out for hours until I'm so hoarse I can hardly talk."

The first part of the digging had gone very well. Now King found it difficult to dispose of the dirt rapidly with his hands.

"Are you all right in there? This is going to take a little while."

"I'm fairly comfortable, if that's what you mean. And I can breathe, thank the Lord! I was afraid at first they were going to bury me and let me die here."

"Who?" asked King.

"I'm not quite sure," said the other. "How do I know who you are?"

Suddenly King stopped his digging.

"We may as well understand each other," he told him. "I'm going to try to get you out. And I give you my word I'm going to help you track down the man that put you in here. But I've got to have your help. If you're willing to give it that'll be fine. If you're not, I may as well stop digging right now!"

"For the love of heaven, don't do that!" pleaded the voice from the grave. "Only I've got to be careful. Maybe I've talked too much already. If you think I'm messed up with some gangsters or rackets you're wrong. This is something different—different from anything you've ever heard before. How did you happen to hear me?"

King went on with his digging as he talked.

King explained and the man in the coffin laughed. Except for the rasping, dry sound of the strange voice it was a rather light-hearted laugh.

"I bet you had a time finding where the sound came from. I never would have gone on a spooky job like that. You see, when I was taken prisoner I had some steel hacksaw blades in my pocket that I'd gotten for a special purpose.

"After I'd laid here for hours and had yelled my head off without anybody coming, I thought of the blades. I could tell by the length of the stovepipe that they hadn't buried me very deep.

"I managed to get out a blade and started it in a crack where the lid doesn't fit quite tight on the box. I was getting along pretty well when I saw your light reflecting in the stovepipe and heard the thud of your feet.

"Then when I didn't hear it any more and the light went out I figured it must have been a car passing."

"Have you any idea where you are?" King asked.

"No," came the answer. "I was in New York City the last I knew. I had a feeling I was being followed. Then I was pulled suddenly into a car and they gagged and blindfolded me. They asked me a lot of questions that I couldn't answer and wouldn't have if I could."

King had finished pulling the dirt from one end of the rough box cover.

"Hold on," he said, "I think I'll have you out in a minute. Then we can talk this over when you're more comfortable." He got up and ran back to the place at the side of the road where he had put the pickaxe. It was gone.

"That's funny," he muttered. He cast his light about the road. "Mighty funny. I'd swear that I dropped that pickaxe right here!" HE SUDDENLY had a sensation of not being alone. He stared about him and flashed the light, but could see no lurking shadows anywhere. Then he straightened and turned back to the place where the man was buried alive.

"Alright," he said, "whoever you are, you've got that pickaxe, but I'll get him out without it."

He ran back to the half-open grave, tore the stovepipe out from its hole.

"Keep your eyes and mouth shut," he said to the man inside. "You may get some dirt in your face for a few minutes."

"Right," mumbled the other.

King clutched at the boards. The feeling that at any moment the mysterious ones who had taken the pickaxe might pounce down upon him drove him on to more frantic efforts.

Board by board the covering came apart. Dirt fluttered down. Then the man who had been buried alive was sitting up. He put head and shoulders through the opening. King got hold of him and pulled. The man struggled with all his might. Then he was lying panting on the pile of sand at the side.

"Quick!" King said. "We've got to get out of here."

He flashed the light on the face of the man. He was young— even younger than King. His face seemed to turn more ashen at King's words as he struggled up to a straight position.

"Of course," he agreed. "Where do we go?"

He stood up. King pushed him down and took him by the arm.

"Don't stand," he whispered. "We've got to keep down as low as these bushes that spot the field, and move as fast—and quietly—as we can."

They moved off doubled over until they were almost on their hands and knees. Now and then King glanced back. Once he thought he could see a dim shadow following. He wasn't sure. He wished he'd thought to turn his lights off on his car. That might have helped some.

He turned to the right. That direction would carry them off into the dimmer shadows. He found it was necessary to half carry the other in order to make good time. It was pitch dark now. He didn't know exactly where they were going. Didn't care.

His only thought was to go silently, then to have time to stop and get a complete explanation from this young man he had saved from a living death.

They must keep going until they were sure they were safe in stopping. Finally they came to a wooded section. There he turned sharply left so that they would pass through the darkest part of the woods.

"Feel better?" he whispered to the young man beside him.

"Yes," came the answer, hoarsely. "The old muscles are getting straightened out. I was pretty well cramped in there for awhile."

"Good!" King hissed. "I thought we would be better off in these woods, but I wish we hadn't tackled it now. We're making more noise than if we'd stuck to the field. Have you any idea who might be following us, if anybody?"

"Not sure," panted the other. "I didn't get a good look at any of them when they jerked me in the car and blindfolded me."

They broke out into the open. The man beside King stood up as they hurried on. King jerked him down again.

"Stay down," he whispered. "If we show ourselves too plainly they might shoot."

They were climbing a slight knoll on the field and had almost reached the top.

Suddenly he fell flat, pulling the young man down beside

11

him. Something like the long slim shaft of an arrow had come swishing through the air, just grazing him.

"What was that?" the young man whispered.

"I don't know," King hissed back. "Something grazed my back from behind."

"They're following us!" exclaimed the other.

"Yes," said King through tight lips.

"I'm going to have a look," said the young man.

King jerked his arm out from under him.

"Better not. Let's wait here for a moment and see what happens. Did you hear that thud right after that thing passed over?"

"No."

"I did," said King. "It was something like a weight striking the ground. Sounds as though it might have been a stone."

"Or perhaps an arrow?" suggested the other.

King turned his head so he faced him fully in the darkness.

"Would an arrow have anything to do with the reason you were buried alive?"

The other thought for a moment.

"It might," he admitted, "although I've not heard of Seminoles using arrows in years."

"Seminoles?" said King. "You mean Seminole Indians?"

"Yes," said the other.

"What have they got to do with it?"

"Nothing—that I know of," said the one beside him. "Except that I come from the everglades section of Florida. That's where the Seminole lives."

## CHAPTER 2
## THE GOLDEN DEATH

F OR A moment King remained motionless. He was listening for the slightest sound and was also studying the place where the other man's face was. He could see it very dimly in the darkness.

Then he whispered a question.

"What brought you up here?"

"Gold," said the other.

King gasped.

"Gold?" Then he almost laughed. "You mean that you came up here to New York to seek your fortune?"

"No," said the other. "The fortune is in Florida. But—" he stopped short.

"Go on," urged King.

Still the young man hesitated.

"I'm not sure that I should tell you this," he said. "I don't know who you are."

"I think possibly you've heard of me," said King.

"I can't think very clearly," said the other. "We're being chased. I've got a hunch that that thing that swished by and made a thud was meant to kill either me or both of us.

"Wouldn't it be better if we got clear of this so that we could talk more freely? I've got to think things out if I'm going to tell this story. And—I'm not so sure whether I should or not."

"Perhaps you're right," said King.

Up to now they had been lying flat on their stomachs. King

raised himself so that he could see fairly well. He swung his head around and tried to make his eyes pierce the darkness behind them. There was nothing there.

Nothing except little clumps of bushes and the grass which rose ten or twelve inches in height.

He flattened himself again and moved a little closer to the other.

"Have you any idea how many might be following us?" he asked.

"No," whispered the other.

"How many were there in the gang that captured you?"

"Two or three," said the young man. "I'm not sure."

"Then," whispered King, "there might be two or three or ten or twelve?"

"Yes," came the low answer. And then: "Have you got a gun?"

"No," said King. "And that's the rottenest luck we've had yet."

Then he thought that over for a moment. This man might be a perfectly innocent person. On the other hand, King might have chanced into some kind of a gang war.

There was no telling what this man might be.

"I think," King whispered, "we've been working on the wrong track here. We've been running in a stooped position so that anyone could pick us out in the dark as we moved. Now we're going to try to get out of this on our stomachs. Right flat down, crawling inch by inch. Steady now. Stay by me. We'll move together without any noise."

They began to move very cautiously on their hands and knees.

Except for a very slight rustle of the grass there was no sound, but they were making very poor headway.

Their lack of speed angered King. He was used to faster motion, still with the danger that lurked out there in the darkness they dared do no better.

They had covered about fifty feet when King stretched out his hand and laid it on the arm of the young man beside him. He had been thinking a lot about what he had said concerning Florida. Couldn't figure anything out of it, but at least it was true that the other had a pronounced southern accent.

The two stopped.

King whispered:

"Hold everything! I'm going to have a look back. You stay down flat."

King raised himself on his elbows just enough to look over the top of the grass.

But it was as it had been before—only tiny clumps of bushes and the grass.

"I think we're making it," King whispered. "Let's keep going."

They crawled on and on until they came to a wall.

"We've got to follow this wall along until we reach a gate or opening," King said. "Then we've got to slide under it. Once around the other side we may stand a better chance of getting away a little faster."

They turned their course and proceeded along the wall, crawling inch by inch as before. The only sound was the gentle rustling of dead grass.

King was about to whisper to the other that they had shaken

off their pursuers when he thought better of it and remained silent.

Foot by foot they crept along that stone wall. It was black as pitch there, except for the light of the stars. They were getting tired of moving in this cramped position. Wouldn't that stone wall ever end? It must have a gate somewhere.

Another hundred feet and then they found it. King's hands touched the posts of a rail stile.

He hissed to the other, "Here we are. Follow me and we'll crawl through."

He reached up for the lowest rail, but there was none. The gate was open. Apparently it hadn't been used in a long time.

They crawled together through the wide opening. The grass and weeds were even taller there than they were in the open field. King felt like leaping to his feet, now that they had found that opening. The suspense wasn't doing his nerves any good. He felt the other trembling a little beside him as they rubbed shoulders.

"Take it easy," King whispered. "We've got a pretty good lead now, I think. But we've got to hold it. We can't take a chance of losing everything now."

"I'm coming all right," whispered the other.

Through and on into the other field now. King pushed himself to the right.

"Let's follow this fence on down," he said. "I think it'll help to shield our movements."

And all that time his heart was pounding rapidly, pulse racing. This suspense was no particular fun. If he only knew what he was fighting, what he was fleeing from, it might help. But there was no chance of that unless he rose up and faced the menace.

And he knew in that case another arrow—or whatever it was—would come whispering through the air like the first had done.

Finally they reached a patch of woods. King stopped to listen and to look behind again. No sound came to his ears. No movement caught his eyes.

If it hadn't been for the disappearance of the pickaxe and the whispering sound with the thud at the end of it, King would have sworn that they were alone.

He heard the breath of the other one coming fast.

"How are you standing it?" King asked.

"I'll make it all right. I'm pretty stiff from this cramped position."

"So am I," said King.

"How much farther will we have to crawl on our stomachs?" the young man asked.

"I don't know. I plan to skirt around the edge of this woods. After we get around it I think we'll be safe in moving upright from there on."

"Good!" the other panted.

They continued their crawling, keeping the woods on their right. Not once after that gentle swishing sound and thud had King heard anything.

Still, he couldn't help feeling that their pursuer was not so far behind. It was like a feeling that some have on entering a dark room where someone is hiding—a presentiment that he was not alone.

They reached the end of that side of the wood and turned down the far side.

HE HEARD the other whispering in a rasping, breathless voice.

"I don't think there's anything following us now. I'm going to take a chance and stand up. I can't stand this crawling forever."

"It won't be forever," King assured him. "Just around the other side of the wood and then we'll get up. We can move faster and more comfortable there. We'll stop here, if you like, until you can catch your breath and rest a little."

"Okay," said the other.

After a few minutes of rest they moved on. They reached the corner of the wood and crept behind a large tree, keeping it between them and the direction from which they had come. They stood up and stretched and leaned up against the tree luxuriously.

"That feel better?" King asked.

"I'll say it does," replied the young man. "You see I was pretty cramped lying in that casket and this crawling business didn't help any."

"Well, we'll stay here and rest a few minutes. That'll give us a chance to stop and listen so we can see if whoever has been trailing us has actually followed us here."

"But how on earth could we be followed?" rasped the other.

"Some people," whispered King, "are very clever at following.

Particularly in the dark. I've met some who are practically cats, as far as seeing clearly in the dark was concerned.

"Now let's stay perfectly still for a few minutes and see if we can hear anything of anyone following us."

They froze there against the tree. There was no sound about them but the gentle breathing of the young man and the soft sighing of the night wind.

King's keen eyes stretched out along the trail in the grass through which they had come. Nothing moved there. Perhaps ten minutes passed. Ho nodded with satisfaction.

"I think that settles it," he said. "I'm guessing that we're O.K. Let's move out into the clear field. I believe it's safe to walk along, bent over."

"Just where are we going?" asked the young man, hesitating a moment longer.

"There's a town back on the main highway about two miles, as I remember," King said. "I've got to find a wrecking truck to come back and get my car. And you can take a bus that'll take you back to New York, if that's where you want to go.

"But the main thing I want to do is find a place where we can feel perfectly safe to talk. I want to learn what this is all about."

"I don't know whether I should tell you or not," the other said, repeating his former words.

"Because you don't know me?" King asked.

"Yes," said the other.

"Have you ever heard of the Secret 6?" King asked.

He heard the other gasp.

"Of course," he said. "Who hasn't? Why, even way down in

Florida, the papers have been full of what the Secret 6 has done up here. We've talked about the whole gang—the Doctor, the Bishop, the Key—and say, that big black Luga—"

"Yes," interrupted King, "we've got a pretty good gang, I guess.

"You'd like to have the Secret 6 helping you on this?" King asked.

"Like it?" said the other. "We'd give anything to have the Secret 6 helping us. I've been to the police with my story. They think I'm crazy."

King smiled in the darkness.

"It sounds as though your case is just the kind we like to work on," he said.

"You mean," gasped the other, "you're one of the Secret 6?"

"Yes. They call me the leader but of course that's not particularly true, because we all work together."

"You mean," gasped the other in amazement, "that you're the one they call King?"

"That's right. But let's go. You'll tell me the story?"

"I should say I would," said the young man. "Yes, let's go."

They stepped out from the shelter of the one large tree and walked in a stooped position, still skirting the woods. For two hundred feet they moved that way. Then King turned a little to the left and that took them out into the open field.

They were walking rapidly now. They had no fear of sound, because anyone who might be following them could follow their movements without the aid of sound.

"This is certainly a streak of luck to find you," said the young man. "Why, my uncle was saying just before I started that he'd like nothing better than to get the Secret 6 working with him on this proposition."

"Your uncle lives in Florida?" King asked.

"Yes. He and Janet, his daughter, live down in Everglades City. In fact, my grandfather founded Everglades City. He moved there a long time ago when my father and uncle were just kids. Since then the town has grown up to be quite a sportsman's paradise.

"You see, grandfather knew where this gold was hidden, but it's going to take a lot of money to get it out."

"Gold?" asked King. "How much gold?"

"About a hundred million," said the other without the slightest inflection in his voice.

"A hundred million?" gasped King.

"Yes," said the young man. "That is, according to the reports that one of my ancestors left to my grandfather. It's buried somewhere around the Ten Thousand Islands. My grandfather spent all his life looking for it. My father and my uncle looked for it too and two or three years ago they found it. The chests, I mean. They're immense. It would take a great deal of engineering equipment to hoist them from the mud where they're buried. That's what I came to New York to see about. There is a prominent New York architect came down to Everglades City for the tarpon fishing last winter. My uncle got to know him very well.

"My uncle operates one of the charter fishing boats there. That's the way he makes his living, and I help him. It takes a crew of two, generally, to handle the boat and the fishing tackle and that sort of thing."

"What's his name?" asked King.

"The same as mine—John Hernando."

"Spanish?" asked King.

"Yes. Spanish ancestry."

"And your father, is he living?" asked King.

"No, he was killed." King could feel the young man shudder. "It was either sharks or alligators. We weren't sure which."

"And you say you came up to New York to find this architect?"

"Yes," said John Hernando. "My uncle and I talked it over for a long time after Mr. Close, that's his name, left his fishing trip at Everglades City. We had him looked up thoroughly and found that he's an absolutely honest man. He's worth a great deal of money.

"But I had hard work locating him when I reached New York. I didn't have his address, and although he had signed his name on the hotel registry we weren't sure of his initials. I stayed in New York several days trying to find him. Then I advertised in one of the papers, but got no reply.

"So I did what was perhaps a foolish thing. I advertised for an honest man who would be willing to invest a small amount of money in order to make several millions. I got several replies and various men came to see me.

"ONE WAS the head of a preparatory school for boys on Long Island. He has his winter school down at St. Petersburg or Tampa. I've forgotten which he said. He seemed to be a very fine man. And he was very anxious to go into the proposition. He said pirate gold had always been a great hobby with him, anyway.

"But about the time we had nearly reached terms one of Mr. Close's friends saw the ad and Mr. Close came to me.

"It seems that he lives in Flushing, Long Island and that's why I couldn't find his name in the city directory."

"Wait a minute," said King. He stopped. They were in the midst of an open stretch of field now, and the lights of the town they were headed for glimmered about a mile away. He looked behind, but there was no sign of movement there.

"I think it would be better," he went on after a moment, "if we stopped right here and got this thing settled. How many other men came to interview you in answer to your ad for an honest man?"

"Five."

"They were all interested in the proposition?" King asked.

"Very much so," said Hernando. "They all wanted to get into it. I suppose there is a fascination about pirate gold for everyone."

"Pirate gold?" said King. "I take it then that one of your ancestors was a member of the pirate crew."

"No," said Hernando. "It was my paternal ancestor who was messed up in the thing at the start. He was a goldsmith in New Orleans. One of the finest craftsmen of his time, I understand.

"According to the story he was commissioned by a stranger to make a small alligator out of gold. This alligator was to go on a golden plate.

"And then there were certain strange figures to go with it. Figures that, in the language the pirate captain would understand, told where the bulk of the gold was hidden. It was, you might say, the key to the hiding place of the treasure.

"This golden plate, with the alligator and the instructions on it, was found years ago up on the Labrador coast. You've heard of the Van Ripkin fortune here in New York?"

"Of course," said King. "Who hasn't?"

"Well, the discovery of this treasure chest with the inscription on it in Labrador was the foundation of it."

"Yes, I've heard so," said King.

"There was about ten million dollars in gold in that one large chest," Hernando said. "But the hundred million is still buried somewhere in the Ten Thousand Islands. My uncle is the only one who knows where it is. Whoever buried me alive was trying to make me tell."

King was thoughtful for a moment. "It looks to me," he said at length, "as though one of these so-called honest men who came to see you in answer to your ad was responsible for your being buried alive."

"I'm sure of it," said Hernando. "But out of the six I can't imagine which one it might be. They all seemed very fine men."

"Who were they?" asked King. "And was there any connection between them, do you think?"

"No, I don't think so," said Hernando. "They all came separately and they were all different types. One was a doctor and one was a lawyer. And then this preparatory-school headmaster or owner; his name was Freeman. He seemed the most likable and the most trustworthy of any of them. He had made a study of buried treasure all his life.

"I can't remember the names of the others offhand. I had them on a slip of paper up in my room at the Altoona Hotel. I had an envelope in the coat pocket of my other suit, and I jotted them down."

"Does the architect, Close, know that he's going to finance the proposition definitely?"

"Yes," said Hernando. "It was while I was leaving his home in Flushing early last evening that I was taken prisoner.

"Someone must have followed me there. And I'm very much afraid that Mr. Close is in for trouble. That was one of the reasons I was trying to escape from the casket, so I could warn him of the possible danger."

"Danger?" said King. "From the same ones who captured you?"

"Yes," said Hernando. "If they know I'm out of the casket and free, I'm afraid they'll go to Close and subject him to torture, thinking he knows where the gold is buried."

"And he doesn't?" asked King.

"No," replied Hernando. "No one will know that until the proper time. Then my uncle will direct operations himself."

"In that case," said King, "I think we'd better notify Close of his danger immediately. Let's get to this town ahead of us as soon as possible. Perhaps we can rent a car there."

He turned to the lights of the Long Island village. Stopped short. Froze in his tracks.

Out of the night came that gentle swishing sound! Soft and low like the flight of an arrow. But now he recognized the difference. It seemed to be throbbing. Throbbing rapidly, but very softly.

King dropped to the ground instantly and as he dropped he

turned to see what was making the sound. He heard a choking cry from John Hernando! Charged toward him as he fell to the ground.

But Hernando was going down even before he caught him, his hands clutching his throat as he fell.

## CHAPTER 3
## DEATH STRIKES AGAIN

THERE WAS a brief struggle, then the writhing body of John Hernando, with the choking sound coming from his lips, twitched and lay still. It was then that King went into action. He remembered the direction that whirling thing had come from. Somewhere out there in the darkness would be the man who had shot or thrown it.

All sense of danger left him now. He must find the man who had discharged that weapon, whatever it was. He didn't take time to figure out what it might be. All he knew was that something had come gently hissing through the air. And had caused either the death or unconsciousness of John Hernando.

King leaped to his feet and charged madly in the darkness in the direction from which the hissing sound had come.

He saw a dark figure leap up out of the grass more than fifty feet away—a lurking form that he could dimly see running in the darkness, bent almost double. King called out a sharp command at the top of his voice.

"Stop or I'll shoot!"

But the man was running like a deer and King was unarmed.

The chief of the Secret 6 had only his bare hands. But he didn't think of that now. His only thought was to reach that fleeing figure and throttle him.

For a moment King thought he was gaining. Then he realized the horrible truth. This man he was chasing was running with the speed of the wind. Even now, after only fifty paces, it was almost impossible to follow the other figure with his eyes.

Moreover, the other ran silently—moved like a shadow.

The fleeing figure came to a high stone wall and leaped it easily. King tried the same thing, but his jumping form wasn't so good—he missed and fell on the other side into a clump of thorny bushes, lacerating his flesh.

He struggled clear and leaped up angrily. He stared about with narrowed eyes for the shadowy form that seemed now almost an apparition.

It was nowhere to be seen!

Up to now he hadn't even heard it once. For a moment he hesitated.

"I'd sure like to get my hands on that bird," he rasped, "but there's no chance of catching him. He can run faster than I can to begin with, and I imagine he'd fight the same way—as fast as lightning. Perhaps I can help Hernando."

He ran back. For some minutes he had difficulty in finding the place where the young man from Florida had fallen. Then he located his still form.

He bent over him, feeling his throat and heart.

King shook his head. There was no heart action.

Then he examined the throat of the young man more carefully. A deep frown creased his brow.

"That's a funny thing," he said half aloud. "Feels like fine wire wrapped around his throat. And it's tight too. That wire has cut right into his flesh. I wonder how—"

He stopped short. His fingers had come in contact with something else. He lifted it up. It was a peculiarly shaped weight that was fastened at one end to the wire about Hernando's throat.

"Say, that's odd," he said. "I wonder if this could be anything like one of those flying garrotes a legionnaire was telling me about one time. Wish I could remember more about it."

He lifted the body of Hernando so that he could unwind the weighted wire from his neck.

"That's funny," he said. "The wire seems to have been tied around his neck. Anyone would think that a magician—"

HE STOPPED again as his hands came in contact with another weight, apparently, exactly like the first one he had found.

In the darkness he could see it gleam. A very dull yellow in the light of the stars. It was the heaviest block of metal for its size he had ever held in his hand.

"These two weights are exactly alike," he said. "And they're fastened together by a length of wire. This wire has been wound and tied around Hernando's neck—no, I'm wrong there—it's been wound, but not tied."

He was unwinding the wire from the other direction now, using the weight on the second end he had found. That unwound easily. Round and round the weight went. He made more than a dozen turns of the wire from Hernando's neck.

When he was through he held up the weights and wire and let Hernando's still form rest back on the ground again.

Holding a weight in each hand he stretched out his arms to their full length. But the wire was much longer than his reach. It was at least nine or ten feet long.

A strange sensation passed over him. It was as though he had found something from another world.

"Yes," he said, "I'll bet this is what that foreign legionnaire told me about." He reached over and felt of Hernando's heart again. "It sure snapped him," he said.

While he made these inspections he watched behind him. Every few seconds his back turned sidewise and he glanced back. That big dark form that he had chased after Hernando had fallen might be coming back to get him.

But it was just as before—though he knew he was being pursued, no sound came.

He got up now. Carried the piece of wire with the strange weights at each end. He said half aloud to himself: "I've got to get to this architect, Close, that Hernando was mentioning."

He strode off across the field. Toward the few lights that were still on in the town. He left Hernando where he had fallen.

He found on entering the town that the street lights were still burning. All the houses and places of business were closed. He went down the main street and found a garage with an apartment above it.

"I'm going to make a guess that the proprietor of the garage lives upstairs," he said.

He felt around in the darkness about his feet. Found some small stones. He tossed them up at the window panes. They rattled and clattered against the glass. He did that several times, waiting between each throwing.

Then suddenly a white figure appeared at the open window and a harsh, woman's voice blasted the night air.

"Get away from there, you drunken bum!" she hurled down at him. "I told you if you went out and got drunk I'd not let you in. If you want to, go to sleep go into the garage with the rest of the wrecks.

"If you come up here while you're drunk I'll break your head with a monkey wrench. A fine husband you turned out to be! Go on, now. Get in the garage. And don't let me hear a word out of you."

King couldn't help but smile. He could see the figure more clearly now. There was the white of a very ample nightgown, and the head of a woman was hanging half out of the window as she shouted her threats. King cleared his throat to answer her.

"Go on," she said, "get in the garage, you dog!"

"I'm sorry to disappoint you, lady," King replied, "but I'm not your husband."

"Huh?" said the woman. "You aren't my husband? Well, what's the idea of coming around and throwing stones at my window at this hour of the morning?"

"I wrecked my car," said King, "two or three miles down the road."

"Oh yeah?" said the woman. "I suppose you're one of them drunken drivers out on a joy ride, eh?"

"Sorry," said King, "wrong again. I'm stone sober. I want to get somebody to go out and tow my car in and fix it as soon as possible. And I'd like to rent a car. I've something very important I've got to do."

"Yeah? Some devilment probably," the woman rasped.

"No," said King. "I've got to save a man's life."

"Oh!" said the woman. "Someone who was hurt in the accident?"

"No," said King, "I was alone. I think I can make you understand if you'll come down, please. And hurry, if you will. I'll pay you well."

"Everybody pays me or they don't get anything done," the woman retorted. "All right. Hold your horses and I'll be down in a minute. Go around in the front and I'll meet you there."

"Okay," said King.

He went around to the front of the building. Waited five minutes. Then he heard the tread of heavy footsteps on the stairs. A light went on.

The door opened and a big, portly woman blinked at him. King blinked back in turn. For this woman was not dressed in the conventional garb of the familiar vogue, but in a large-sized monkey suit of coveralls.

"You see," King said, "I'm a detective. I was running down a crime when my car was wrecked two or three miles down the highway. It's there where I hit a culvert. I've learned something that I wanted to know, and I've got to get back to save a man whom I don't believe realizes he's in danger."

"Detective?" asked the woman. "Well, my goodness sakes alive! Why didn't you say so in the first place? Why, say, I got a brother in New York that's a policeman. John Flynn is his name. He patrols a beat up around 189th street. You must know him if you're a detective."

KING FEIGNED astonishment.

"Oh you're John Flynn's sister?

"Why, sure, I know Johnny. That's fine. And now about a car? Have you got a car you can rent me?"

"Well, I don't know whether you'd call it a car or not," the old woman said. "It's an old buggy but it runs good. I keep cars that way. And then I've got the tow there. But of course if you want me to go out there and get your wreck I'll have to take the tow car myself. Or did you want to go with me?"

"No, I've got to get the other car and be going. I'll leave a deposit on the car if you wish."

"A deposit nothing!" said the woman. "Any friend of my brother Johnny, I'd trust anywhere."

"Thank you," said King, trying not to smile too broadly. "And about my wreck. One side of the front axle is gone. I imagine you'll have to put in a whole new front end. I presume you'll have to wait for your husband to get back before that can be done."

"What?" snapped the woman. "My husband to fix the car? Say, he don't know nothing about automobiles. He tried to make me think he did once so he could get the money that my Aunt Tilly left to start this business with.

"But that loafer! He can't stay sober ten minutes. Why, there wouldn't be any work done around here if I didn't do it. And believe me, when Katie Marshall fixes a car it's fixed. You ask anybody."

King smothered a chuckle and a cough.

"Yes," he said. "I can imagine so."

The woman was unlocking the garage now. King started forward to help her open the doors. But Katie Marshall needed no help from anyone. She switched on the lights.

"There," she said, pointing to an old flivver with flopping fenders. "You can take that car. It doesn't look like much but it'll take you there and get you back. And I'll go right out and tow your wreck in and start working on it."

King glanced about the garage.

"You'll have to wait until sometime tomorrow for parts, won't you?"

The woman hesitated. "What kind of a car is it?"

King told her the make of the light sedan. She glanced around the garage.

"Like that one?" pointing to one similar to the sedan of the Secret 6.

"If it's nothing but the front end gone," she said. "I'll have your car fixed up by morning."

King stared at her. "You mean take the front end out of that car?" he asked.

"Sure," she said. "Why not? You're a friend of Johnny's and that car's in here for three or four days. Old man Johnson owns it and he wouldn't have nobody else but me work on his car. He won't care. I'll take his whole front out and then put the new part in his—if that's all right with you."

"It sure is," said King, "if I can get it in the morning when I come back."

"You can," she said. And she said it with her jaws thrust forward, as though she defied the whole world to stop her. "You take the flivver," she continued, "and I'll go and get the wreck. The key's in the flivver."

"Thanks," said King. "Thanks a lot."

He went over and climbed into the car with the flapping fenders, started the motor and drove out of the garage toward Flushing.

He chuckled to himself as he drove.

"Boy! I'd like to see that husband of hers," he said aloud. "I'll bet he's a honey. The bird must have nerve, though, to step out and go places with that battle-ax waiting for him. I'll bet she can fix an automobile, too."

He felt the wire and weights in his pocket.

As yet he hadn't had a chance to look at them in the light. He didn't take the time now, because he was driving toward Flushing with the flivver wide open, and it took all of his attention to keep the car on the road.

It was still dark when he reached the city. He found only a lunch wagon open and a night police officer inside talking to the proprietor.

"I'm looking," he said, "for a Mr. Close. He's an architect and I have to see him at once on something very important. Could you tell me where he lives?"

"Close?" said the cop. "Close?"

"Sure, you know," said the proprietor. "He's got that château place on the Manhasset Road."

"Oh, yeah," said the cop. "Sure, I remember. Well, you go out toward Manhasset about two miles. And you know what one of those châteaux look like?"

King nodded. "Yes, I've lived in them."

"Oh, you was over across too?" asked the cop. "What outfit?"

"Twenty-second pursuit squadron," he answered before he thought. "About three miles out?"

"That's right," said the cop. "Me, I was in the 27th Division and Jimmie here that runs the lunch wagon was my corporal."

King nodded.

"Great war, wasn't it?" he said. "I'll be seeing you."

He went out and climbed in the car again. Found a sign that pointed toward Manhasset and pulled the throttle lever down as far as it would go. It was getting daylight now. He could see the houses very plainly in the gray of dawn.

He glanced at the speedometer but it wasn't working. He guessed at two miles and began watching for the château of the great architect.

A few minutes later he found it and slowed down. The place looked like a château alright. The architect's designing was superb. There were two round towers with long high French windows. Sloping lawns stretched away from a great paved court.

KING TURNED in at the drive. There was nothing alarming about the place. Only peace and quietness seemed to dwell there. No hint of danger.

"I wonder," he said, half aloud, "if anybody's up at this hour."

He had just uttered that as he swung up the drive. His eyes were roving across the front of the palatial home. He stopped and focused his glance on one of the high French doors that opened on the paved court in front.

The curtains had moved. Someone had peered out. The curtains went back in place again.

Then, as King stopped the old car directly in front of the steps, the French door opened and a man clad in a dressing gown stepped out on the open veranda.

He walked toward King with a quick step. He was about fifty and of medium build. He was bareheaded and his hair was gray at the sides. He had an air about him that gave him a distinguished look.

"You're Mr. Close?" King asked when they met at the top of the steps. "Mr. Close, the architect?"

The other nodded. "Yes, but I'm afraid you have the advantage of me. I don't recall having seen you before."

King studied him for a moment.

"Mr. Close, you look like a very sane sort of person. I think I'll tell you who I am so that you'll understand before I get any deeper in the matter."

The architect smiled. "I'm glad," he said, "that you feel you can trust me." There was the very slightest tinge of sarcasm in his voice.

"Mr. Close," King went on, "you've heard of the Secret 6, perhaps?"

"Of course. We hear many things for and against the Secret 6."

"Things for them, from the people with whom they have dealt, and things against them from the police who do not understand them?"

Close smiled.

"Yes," he said, "I think that measures it up pretty well."

"Then," said King, "I think I may tell you who I am. I'm known as King, one of the Secret 6."

Close opened his mouth, stared for an instant, then smiled.

"Well, this certainly is a pleasure," he said. "But just what is it that brings you here—and particularly at this hour of the morning?"

"I was just going to ask you," King said, "what got you up so early."

Close hesitated.

"Oh," he said, "I suppose I may as well tell you—if you're who you say you are. There's a little deal I seem to be messed up in. It's one of those things, you know, King, that we've all rather dreamed of as kids. But we're always sure that nothing like it would happen to us."

King nodded.

"Yes, I've always wanted to find some pirate gold myself!"

Close frowned.

"How in the name of Time did you know?"

"I assure you it was more than a guess on my part. I have just left John Hernando—or perhaps I should say, his body. He was killed while I was talking to him."

The square-cut face of the architect blanched. "Killed!" he repeated. "Why, I can't understand. He was here with me just last evening. Where's his body?"

King jerked his head toward the east.

"Back in the field where he fell. It's about twenty miles from here."

"Good Lord! That's too bad. But I can't imagine who—"

"Neither can I. That's what we're trying to find out."

Close half turned toward the door.

"You haven't had breakfast have you? It's rather early, but I thought I might eat, and I'd be happy to have you join me."

"I'd be more than glad to," said King. "I'm pretty hungry."

"Good. I'll order it served out here on the court. Excuse me for a moment."

The sun was peeping up over the eastern horizon as he came back, followed by a butler who carried a table which he sat at the edge of the court overlooking the great lawn.

He arranged two chairs, one on either side of the table. Close motioned King to one and took the other himself. Then, while the butler busied himself serving the breakfast, King began.

"Perhaps you'd get a better idea of the whole situation if I started at the beginning and told you what's happened to me."
WHEN HE had finished Close was thoughtful.

"This flying garrote that killed Fernando—what is it?" he asked.

"I wouldn't have known myself," said King, "if a legionnaire that had been in Senegal, West Africa, hadn't told me once. He says there's a group of negroes there—I don't know whether they're headhunters or not—who use this weapon in open country.

"It's a very long wire or very stout cord or thong eight or ten feet long. It has equal weights of several ounces at each end of it.

"They throw it by taking a hold of one of the weights and whirling the other around and over their heads. Something like they used to whirl a sling in ancient times.

"When they let go of it it whirls through the air, and they can make a direct hit, this legionnaire told me, at one hundred and fifty and sometimes two hundred feet."

"But how does it work?" asked Close.

"The trick," King said, "is to aim it straight enough so that some part of the wire strikes the man you're aiming at somewhere in the neck. That stops the forward movement of the wire, but the two weights keep on revolving. They whirl round and round his neck in opposite directions with terrific tension. The man is almost instantly choked to death."

Close gasped.

"And this is what happened to Hernando?" he demanded.

"Yes."

Close's eyes narrowed.

"Hew do you know?"

"For several reasons," King replied. "For one thing I was with him when it happened, and for another I have the flying garrote that killed him here in my pocket. As a matter of fact, this is the first time I've had a chance to take it out and look at it in the light."

He took it from his pocket. The eyes of Close fastened on it even before King saw it himself.

"Gold!" he shouted. "The whole thing is gold!"

King stared down at the coil of fine wire and the two peculiarly shaped weights in his hand.

"Say, that's interesting," he observed. "The whole thing is gold. The wire and—by George! Look at these weights."

He glanced up at Close and the architect's face was a bit ashen.

"The Golden Alligator!" he gasped.

King frowned and glanced again at the weights. He had known that they were strangely shaped when he touched them in the darkness. Now he saw. Close had spoken the truth.

Each weight resembled a rather stocky little alligator about three inches long from tail to snout. The wire was fastened to each through a small hole in the tail. He eyed Close speculatively.

"Yes," he said. "They're golden alligators. Here—feel them. They're certainly heavy enough to be solid gold. But why anybody is running around Long Island, throwing gold away, is more than I can understand. They could use lead just as well as gold."

Close moved nervously.

"I'm afraid you don't understand," he said. "There's quite a story connected with this golden alligator business."

The butler had finished bringing the breakfast to the table. Now he bowed and stood at the side.

"Is there anything else?" he asked.

Close shook his head without even looking at the food before him.

"No. That will be all. You may go."

When the butler was gone, the architect lighted a cigarette instead of beginning to eat.

"Apparently," he began, "you've never heard of the group who operated at one time under the name of the Golden Alligator. The queer part is, that it has to do with a buried treasure."

"This same buried treasure?" asked King.

"I rather suspect so. It is the same treasure, if Hernando knew what he was talking about.

"The only story I've ever heard stated that the famous Captain Kidd, whose real name was Kidder, had a half-brother whom he took with him on his expeditions. This half-brother was always jealous of the famous captain and plotted to kill him several times but always waited until they got more gold.

"ANYWAY, THROUGH some slip-up, he learned where Kidd buried part of his treasure. Of course we all know that Kidd was hung. As I understand it it was the half-brother who betrayed him.

"At any rate Kidd's half-brother formed a secret organization called the Golden Alligator, because it was by this symbol with the inscription on the Labrador chest, that anyone who knew the right key could locate the hidden treasure. And only Kidd himself knew the place."

"There is one thing I can't figure out, Close," said King. "I understand from what Hernando tells me that this gold is buried somewhere in the Ten Thousand Islands off the southwest coast of Florida.

"But I also understand that it will take quite a lot of money for engineering equipment to salvage it. Those chests must be tremendously heavy. How could Captain Kidd bury them by himself?"

Close laughed a little less nervously for the moment. For now King could see he was really interested in the story he was telling.

"I guess we didn't know Captain Kidd very well. And probably a good thing we didn't," said Close. "It is said that he took several of the strongest men in his crew to help him bury the gold and killed them afterward."

King nodded thoughtfully. "I see," he said. "Then the bones of those men might help us locate the treasure!"

Close shook his head. "I imagine Kidd was foxier than that. He probably killed the men some distance away. Or maybe he just set them to drift in a leaky boat. There are many ways of getting rid of men at sea without leaving any evidence."

Close began to eat now.

"You plan, I take it to go on with this venture?" King queried.

"Certainly. I'll help Hernando get that gold out, if I have to spend every nickel I have in the world."

"Do you still think," asked King, "that this group started 200 years ago by Kidder's half-brother under the name of the Golden Alligator is still functioning?"

"I'm positive of it," said Close. "It must be some descendant of that half-brother or of his organization that is carrying the thing on."

He pointed to the fine wire and the heavy gold alligator at each end.

"Take a look at that," he went on. "That ought to give you your answer."

King shook his head.

"This whole thing is hard to believe," he said.

"I doubt I would have believed it myself if I hadn't seen what's happened so far," said Close. "You're going to help see this thing through?" And there was concern in his voice.

"Try and stop me!" said King. "All my life I've wanted to be mixed up with some buried treasure. I guess every kid has. Well, now, believe me, we're going to carry this thing out if it's humanly possible. There's one murder to even up right from the start and I'm afraid there's going to be—"

Suddenly his chair tilted back. He ducked behind the stone parapet of the open paved veranda. At the same time he shot his right foot under the table straight for the chair of the architect.

"Look out!" he yelled.

That same soft swishing sound had come to him again from behind some shrubs that dotted the magnificent lawn.

Close pitched over backwards as his chair fell before King's kicking foot. There in the shelter of the parapet King was trying to see him under the table. He saw his struggling and he heard a choking sound.

# CHAPTER 4
# PURSUIT

FROM HIS position King couldn't see clearly under the table. But he knew only too well the answer to that choking sound he had heard.

The flying garrote had struck again!

He leaped to his feet now and stared out across the lawn. He did that barely in time to catch sight of a figure racing from one clump of bushes to another. It looked like the silhouette of the one he had chased in the darkness a few hours before. But he got a little better look at the man than he had in the dark.

The instant King saw him, he leaped over the stone railing and ran headlong after him. The man had broken into a thicker clump of shrubbery in the corner of the estate. And there were a few tall trees there too.

That was the last King saw of him. Then he heard the sound of a car engine out on the highway that passed the house. King broke out into the open just in time to see the rear of the car vanish around a turn. It was a large closed car. That was all he could tell about it.

He stood still, panting. His brain was going around a bit dizzily. He turned quickly and retraced his steps back to the veranda of the Close château.

The butler was there, bending over his master. He rose and with a quick glance at King went hurriedly back into the house. King dropped to his knees beside the still form of Close. There about the architect's neck was a garrote—like the one lying on the table! Golden alligators formed each end of the wire.

Swiftly he unwound the weighted wire from around Close's neck. As had been the case with young John Hernando, the wire had cut deeply into the flesh. So deeply that in one place the skin was lacerated and blood oozed out.

King worked for a few moments over the prostrate man, trying his best to revive him with artificial respiration, but heart action had stopped. Close was dead.

He rose quickly, reached for the other flying garrote that was still lying on the table.

He and Close had been discussing it when the sudden end had come. Then he heard footsteps from the open French door.

"I've 'phoned for the police, sir," the butler said.

King hesitated for a moment. He turned slowly.

"Who told you to?" he demanded. Then he shrugged. "Well, I don't suppose it matters. At the rate this is going they'll be in on the case before long, anyway."

As he spoke he picked up the second garrote to put it in his pocket. But the butler's voice snapped out an order. "If I were you," he said, "I'd not put that in my pocket, sir. Because if you do, this gun I have in my hand might go off!"

King stared—stared straight into the muzzle of a nasty little automatic that the butler held.

"What's the idea?" he demanded.

"I'm not sure, sir," said the butler. "But it would appear to me that you had something to do with the death of Mr. Close, sir."

"Something to do with Close's death?" explained King. "Why,

you crazy idiot, that's why I came here. To try to warn him he was in danger."

"All I know," insisted the butler stubbornly, "is what I've seen and overheard. I believe the police can handle it better now."

King's eyes narrowed.

"Do you mean to say," he demanded, "that you're going to hold me here until the police come?"

"Yes, sir," said the butler. And there was a mean tilt to his jaw as he said it.

King was thinking hard, trying his best to figure a way out. Then he shrugged.

"Okay," he said, "if that's the way you feel about it. But you might have the decency to throw a blanket over your master. I suppose you wouldn't permit him to be moved until the police get here?"

"No, sir," he said, "I want them to see him exactly as he fell. They'll be here any minute."

There was no doubt that the butler meant business. He was faithful to his master and had plenty of nerve. King knew that he couldn't bluff him out of the affair; knew that he'd shoot at the first false movement.

But neither could King stay there if the police were coming.

"You wouldn't mind if I sat down?" he asked.

"No, sir," the butler said. "Not at all, sir."

King sat down in the same chair that he had occupied before. It had been tipped over in the confusion. In straightening it and bringing it up so he could sit in it, he moved it closer to the butler, who stood motionless.

But that gun in his hand was trained on King constantly. And King must get out! The police, if they captured him, would doubtless hold him for the murder of Close. Anything he might say would be laughed at.

HE WAS sitting perhaps five feet away from the butler. He measured the distance from his right foot to the gun.

His brain spun as he tried to think of something. Then he turned his head side-wise and looked down toward the end of the paved terrace. His face lighted. There was nothing coming from that direction, but he must make the butler think that there was to divert his attention.

King became suddenly alert as though he were noticing something down there.

"Oh! Here the police come now," he said. "Funny that they'd come over the end of the—"

He never finished the sentence—it wasn't necessary. His two hands clutched the arm of the chair. His body, balanced by his left foot on the paving, shot forward, feet first.

The moment that the butler had turned his head, King's right foot came up in a perfectly aimed kick. The butler was just turning back with a look of alarm when King's toe struck his wrist with brutal force.

The gun flew from his grasp, and the butler clutched his injured wrist with a groan of pain. He threw his legs around the legs of the butler, locked them, and hurled him to the paving.

He reached for the gun, but the butler was nearer—closer to where it had fallen. He too was trying to get it and they struggled and fought there to get it, rolling over and over.

The butler delivered a vicious kick that landed in King's stomach. For a moment it knocked him out—but only for a moment. Just as the butler was touching the gun with his finger tips King jerked him away.

King was closer now. King made a move to grasp it. The butler lunged. Instantly King changed his movements.

He ducked sidewise. Weaved backwards. And then shot his body forward again. And when he leaped, his right fist shot like a projectile to the jaw of the butler.

*Crash!*

The butler's head snapped back. His knees buckled. King caught him as he fell to keep his head from striking the paving and causing a possible brain concussion.

He laid him down gently. Someone was running from the French door. He didn't turn to see who it was. He ducked for the gun that was still lying on the stones. Then, the pistol in his hand, he wheeled. Even before he saw the figure he heard the scream of a girl. A young woman, dressed in the garb of a maid, froze there. She screamed again.

"If it's the butler you're worried about," King said, "he'll be around shortly. He's not hurt. I'll have to go now."

"You villain! You murderer!" screamed the girl.

King didn't wait for any more. He ran down the steps, leaped into the flivver with a prayer that it would start. That Katie Marshall knew how to keep these old wrecks going.

The engine did start—with a bang and a rattle. Then he was rolling out of the grounds at top speed. He turned out on the main highway and toward the village where his own car should be waiting by now.

The throttle lever came down as far as it would go. King was leaning forward, pushing on the wheel, trying to get all the speed out of it he could. But a scant forty-five was all she would do and with plenty of argument at that.

He rolled out of that settlement and into another. Kept looking back to see whether he was being followed. He thought just before he made the first bend on the main highway that he saw a car turn in the Close place. He couldn't be sure.

Now he stared back for what seemed the hundredth time. A car was coming and it was coming at top speed, too. It looked like a police car—a small, fast touring car with the top down. It was gaining on him plenty down the long stretch behind.

He sighted a wood just ahead. A section that he guessed covered a square mile or more of land. The growth was thick and would do for hiding for a moment.

He jammed on the brakes and pulled the car over in the ditch. The police car was gaining like lightning. He smiled as an idea came to him.

His hand went up to the switch and he removed the key. Then with that firmly in his pocket he ran headlong into the woods. He had gone perhaps a hundred yards, when he heard the wild scream of brakes. He heard also the shout of a police officer.

"Stop! Or we'll fire."

He knew that was just bluff—because they couldn't see him. King ran on. He could hear the crashing of twigs and branches as the police tore into the woods.

They couldn't know definitely which way he had taken. He made a sharp right turn and ran for all he was worth. Doubled over. He was running parallel to the road now. He could hear the police coming on at his right.

Then as he raced farther towards the west he heard them crashing behind him. They had missed him completely, but he must be careful. They were covering a wide area of the woods.

A little farther on he turned to the right again and headed back toward the road where the old flivver and the faster police car were parked. He reached the edge of the wood and crouched and listened.

He heard the heavy feet of the officers combing the woods for him.

*Crash! Crash! Crash!*

About two hundred yards to the east he could see the police car.

He grinned for the second time.

"If I make this I'm going to be good," he said. "And with luck I'll make it. Boy! What a surprised bunch of cops they'll be when they find their car is—"

HE STOPPED short. Ducked back instantly into the woods. He had seen a figure near the police car. They had left one of the officers to guard the car.

His nimble brain began working on that proposition. Then an idea came that might possibly work.

He crept noiselessly along the border of the woods, just under cover. He could hear the police threshing about very distantly.

They were far to the rear of the woods. He peered out of his screen of leaves only fifty yards away from the police car.

He saw the officer who had been left on guard sitting there on the running board.

King circled back into the woods until he came to a place eighty or a hundred yards back, directly opposite the two cars.

He could hear the other police far on the other side of the woods now and he felt safe in trying his experiment.

He shouted in a deep voice.

"Hey, you in the car! Come on and help us look for this guy. What do you think we brought you on this trip for—just to sit around and warm that running board?"

He heard the other answer him.

"I got to stay and watch the car so that guy doesn't drive it off."

"That's a lousy excuse," King yelled from behind a bush. "Take the key out and bring it along. He won't be able to drive it without that."

He tensed now and listened for the answer.

"Okay," said the cop rather reluctantly, and King heard him walking leisurely through the undergrowth.

King skirted that area as quietly as he could, went around to the left and circled far enough from the advancing police officer to avoid being heard or seen.

He heard the cop pass his position and call.

"Where are you?"

King made a cup of his hand and shouted back into the deeper woods from which he had come.

"Back here. Straight ahead of you. I can hear you coming."

"Okay," said the other lazily moving on.

King crept to the edge of the road and inspected his position more carefully. He was within twenty or thirty feet of the two cars.

He heard the rumble of a truck along the highway. Another car passed, they shutting out any sound that the police might make. He must move fast now—They might be coming back any minute.

He stepped out on the road and walked boldly toward the police car. It was only a few steps. But there was plenty of suspense in that walk—any moment a bullet might tear out of the woods, aimed at him.

He felt a little easier when he reached the left hand side of the car. There he lifted the hood silently. Ducked down so anyone coming out of the woods wouldn't see him.

He clutched the wires that ran from the distributor to the spark plugs. Yanked hard on them. They stayed fast. He yanked again with all his might and this time they came out. After lowering the hood he walked to the old flivver. He still carried the wires in his hand.

"They'll have a sweet time starting that again with these gone," he said to himself.

He climbed in the flivver, put his key in the switch and stepped on the starter. There was a loud rasping grinding sound. Then a bang and the engine started. And at that moment he heard shouts from the woods!

The flivver shot forward rattling into top speed. He couldn't hear the shouts but now he could hear shots. He crouched there at the wheel. Turned and looked back. Two cops were standing in the road, taking aim at him!

He swerved the flivver back and forth to throw them off. He came to a bend in the road, and looking back a second time he saw the cops waving their arms and shouting towards the woods as they ran back toward their car.

Once around the bend King came to a dirt road. He turned instantly and shot down it. The road was rough and the flivver leaped and bucked like a wild mustang.

But he kept going. Managed to hold her in the road. Wished for more speed. He came to a left fork in the dirt road and took it.

That would take him generally toward the town where he had gotten the car. He could reach it as well that way as he could on the main highway, he thought.

He slowed now as not to cause any suspicion with his enormous forty-five miles an hour.

SOMETIMES THERE was a question of which road he should take. But he let the morning sun guide him and turned always generally east toward the village. Once he found that a turn on the dirt road brought him out on the main highway again. He swerved and turned back, took the next turn to the left, and kept on.

He knew that the tearing of the ignition wires from the policemen's car would hold them up, but not for long. They'd step out on that main highway and commandeer another car for their purpose.

He saw a sign indicating that the town he was aiming for

was only two miles away. It was only a few minutes after that that he came into the town and pulled up in front of the garage.

The doors were open so he drove in. A blinking, blurry-eyed little man leaning against the back of a car stared at him.

"Say," he said, "where'd you get that car?"

King opened his mouth to answer. But the big woman who had answered his call the night before bellowed from under a car in the rear of the garage.

"You keep your nose out of this. Who is it?"

Then King saw her squeezing her portly form out from under the car on a coaster and he recognized the car as the light sedan of the Secret 6.

The woman spied him. She was puffing a little as she got to her feet.

"Oh," she said, "it's you. You're back again. Have any trouble with the car?"

"Not a bit," said King. "It ran like a top."

"I knew it would," she said. "There ain't nobody that can keep a car running better than Katie Marshall."

"How's my car coming?" King asked.

"I'm just finishing it," she said. "I got about three more bolts to tighten and you can drive it away."

"That's fine," said King.

She slid down under the front of the car again. Worked there for a few minutes while King lighted a cigarette. Then she came out.

"There," she said. "Get in and back her out and turn her around and see how she works."

The car seemed to work and steer perfectly.

"You certainly know this automobile business," King complimented her.

"It's a good thing somebody knows something around here," the woman said. "If I left it to my husband there, holding up the back of that car, we'd all be starving to death."

"Now, Katie," the husband said. "That ain't a nice way to talk."

The woman bristled.

"Well, you just try to keep me from talking any way I want to and see what happens!"

"Oh, now," said the husband, "you know I wouldn't do that, Katie."

"You're right. You wouldn't."

"Look at him," she continued to King. "Don't he look like a fish that's been swimming around in a globe of alcohol all night?"

King tried to avoid a direct answer.

"How much is my bill altogether?" he asked.

"Well," she said. "The flivver—I'll only charge you for the gas. How far did you go?"

"I'm not sure," said King. "About forty or fifty miles, I think."

"Let's see," said the woman. "Forty or fifty miles. That's about two and a half or three gallons of gasoline. Say three, and that'll cover the oil. We'll make it about seventy-five cents for that.

"And that front end job. I guess I can straighten some of them parts so they'll do for the old man's car. He don't drive over twenty miles an hour.

"And I've been working since around three o'clock. That's a

dollar an hour. That'd be about five dollars there. Oh, now, let's see—"

The jangle of the telephone interrupted her ponderous thoughts. The husband leaned away from the back of the car he seemed to be holding up and walked to the telephone that hung on the wall. He must have had a presentment. For at the same time his portly wife snapped, "Answer that 'phone!" he took down the receiver.

"Hello," he said.

"Well, let's see," the woman said. "Five dollars for time. And seventy-five cents for use of the flivver. And—"

"Holy gee," the husband cut in. "Hey, it's the police calling and they—"

## CHAPTER 5
## WANTED: AN HONEST MAN

THE BIG woman whirled on her little husband. "Shut up!" she barked. "Can't you see I'm trying to figure? Now let's see. Five seventy-five plus—There was a new tire and a new wheel and I had a spare one that somebody found. So I guess I can let you have that whole thing for ten dollars. And—"

"But listen, Katie," the husband pleaded. "The police are calling and they say they found a car with numbers that—"

The woman spun round. She crouched with surprising speed and when she came up she held a large monkey wrench in her hand that she had picked up from the running board of a nearby car.

And she bellowed again at her husband.

"If I hear another word out of you I'm going to wrap this monkey wrench around your neck so tight that you'll choke to death. Always bla-bla-blain' and you never say anything. And here I am trying to figure this man's bill and you keep butting in all the time."

"Yes, but Katie," pleaded the man. "The—"

The woman advanced toward him. Raised the monkey wrench with such savagery that for a moment King, trying to keep from laughing, thought he was about to see a murder committed right before his eyes.

"So help me!" cried the woman. "If you don't shut up I'm going to—"

"Alright," said the man with a shrug. "But don't come around telling me I got you into trouble."

"Now, let's see," said the woman, "where was I? Five-seventy-five, and ten dollars for that wheel and tires and then the whole front end job.

"Now, Bill Smith said he put in a front end once about a year ago and I think he said the parts was something like fifteen dollars altogether. Would that be all right with you, Mister? I'll let you off cheap, of course, seeing as how you know my brother."

"Anything you say," said King. "That'll be a little over thirty dollars. Here—" He stuffed four ten-dollar bills into her hand. "If that's satisfactory that'll pay you for your extra service."

"Well, now, that certainly is fine of you," the woman said. "And you tell my brother when you see him that you met me, won't you? Let's see. What's your name, mister?"

"Murphy," replied King.

"And that's a good name, too," she said.

King was climbing into his car. The husband was still holding the 'phone receiver.

"Katie, you better come over and talk to these guys yourself," he said.

She beamed at King. And as he drove out he saw her take the receiver and speak into the mouthpiece. He grinned as he pressed the throttle down to the floor. And he sincerely hoped that she had done a good job on the front end of his car. Because at the speed he was going to drive back to the cabin of the Secret 6 he'd need all the safety he could get. He headed for New York. That would give Katie Marshall and her husband a chance to tell the police that he had gone that way. At the west edge of the village he turned off on a dirt road.

Looking back he saw a car with four cops tearing into town from the west. He smiled as he turned on another dirt road that took him around the outer edge of the village.

A few minutes later he came upon the main highway to the east and drove on at top speed.

Yes, the front end seemed to be holding up nicely. The car steered as well as it ever had. The speedometer climbed to sixty and then to seventy.

He left it there. There wasn't any need of running the chance of being picked up by a state trooper for making eighty-five or ninety miles an hour, and he was careful to slow up going through small towns.

Sometime later he reached the mass of woods where the cabin

"Here it is," King said. "The names of the six honest men."

was hidden on the south shore of the Sound. He saw that the road was clear in each direction and turned into the bedrock drive. After parking the car in its usual hiding place at the end of the hidden drive he struck off down toward the cabin.

The giant black form of Luga loomed in front of the door as King broke into the tiny clearing. The negro was carrying a great armful of wood.

"Master!" the faithful Zulu chief cried. "You back all right? We worry about you. Think maybe something happen to you."

As they entered the cabin together the Bishop took his meerschaum pipe from his lips. His merry eyes twinkled.

"Yes, indeed. We're very glad to see you. We were just wondering what might be keeping you."

"Anything happen to the car?" asked the Doctor who was standing by the big fireplace.

The Key with his bent nose grinned rather crookedly. "Aw, don't ask the guy so many questions," he said. "He probably had a heavy date that he doesn't want to talk about."

"Or perhaps," ventured Shakespeare, the old actor, "you stayed over for a late show?"

"Doctor," King said, "you come the closest of anyone. Something did happen to the car. But that can't be compared to what happened afterward. I've run into one of the strangest situations I've ever heard of."

"What was she? Blonde or brunette?" chuckled the Key.

"That'll do," said the Bishop, although his eyes still held a slight twinkle.

"This is a pretty serious proposition," said King. "Maybe you'll get the idea, Key, when I tell you that since I wrecked the car on a culvert two men have been murdered."

"What! Only two?" grinned the Key. "Kind of a slow night for you, wasn't it?"

THE BISHOP turned suddenly grave.

"Key," he said, "will you kindly refrain from interrupting again? I'm sure we all want to know what King has seen."

"Okay," said the Key. "I'm sorry."

King grinned at him then turned to the others.

"How would you all," he asked, "like to investigate a case concerned with buried treasure? The treasure of Captain Kidd."

"How much?" asked the Key.

"Would a hundred million dollars be enough to interest you?"

The Key jumped to his feet. "A hundred million!" he exclaimed. "Phew. Say, listen. You go ahead and tell your story, fella. For a hunk of a hundred million I'd keep my mouth shut until the end of the world."

"Okay," said King. "Then here's what's happened."

He related his adventures, and when he had finished the Key was the first to speak.

"I get it," he said. "This guy, Kidd, left the ten million as a sort of bait for the other hundred million. And if someone found the ten million and guessed right about the inscription on the top of the chest, then maybe with a lot of luck he could find the hundred million?"

"Yes," said King. "That's the way I understand it. Van Ripkin probably didn't suspect the inscription meant anything. But young Hernando's ancestor, the goldsmith, must have figured it out. That is, he figured out the general location, but not the exact spot. And that, beyond doubt is why, almost a hundred years later, one of his descendants, young John's grandfather, settled in Everglades City—to hunt the treasure."

King took the two golden garrotes from his pocket and laid them carefully on the table.

"Take a look at these," he said. "Maybe that'll make you realize there's something to it. Each of those little wires killed a man!"

The five men leaned forward eagerly, studied the weapons with interested scrutiny. The Bishop was the first to speak.

"But how?" he demanded. "Those weights don't look heavy enough to crush a man's skull."

Before King could answer, Luga had stretched out a massive hand and picked up one of the loops. He examined it thoughtfully, a puzzled frown on his face.

"Luga think he know," he said presently. "Some Senegalese use them in West Africa. Weapon kills at distance of almost hundred yards."

"How are they thrown?" King asked.

"There was Senegalese chief in school with me at Capetown," said Luga. "He tell me how they work one time. You take hold of one weight and swing other weight at end of wire or rope or thong round head very fast. Then let go and throw at enemy. Wire catch him around neck and weights swing both ways. Big man throw one with enough weight and very fine wire can almost cut small man's neck off."

"Nice little party," King said.

"Yes," said Luga. "Government stop use now. Against the law."

King nodded. "I imagine it would be against the law over here if they knew about it."

"You say that John Hernando was killed with one of these?" the Doctor asked.

King nodded. "And so was Close, the architect. I'd heard of them myself. They call them flying garrotes in the foreign legion."

"Jolly!" said the Bishop suddenly. "I saw that ad young Hernando put in the paper. Wait. I'll get it."

He started looking through the want-ad section of the New York newspaper, and when he had located it, read the advertisement aloud.

"Wanted—an honest man who is willing to invest between twenty and thirty thousand dollars for a fifth share in a hundred million dollars of buried treasure.—See John Hernando, Altoona Hotel."

"Jolly!" the Bishop chuckled as he laid down the paper. "That makes me think of the old story of Diogenes going about with a lantern looking for an honest man."

THE DOCTOR moved restlessly. "Well, what do we do next?" he asked.

"I think the Key and I will go on the next trip," said King. "We want to find out who these six men are who answered the ad."

The Bishop smiled. "I should imagine that he'd have half of New York in his lap for an ad like that."

King shook his head.

"You, Bishop, with your trusting disposition, probably wouldn't realize the fact that there are wild schemes like this running in the paper every now and then. It's surprising how many of them do get answered when you consider how many people have been stuck."

He got up, turned to the Key. "You want to go with me?"

"Sure," grinned the Key. "You can count me in on a cut of the hundred million any old time."

King paused and turned to face the dapper little man. "Listen, Key," he began gravely. "The chances are we may never get a nickel out of that hundred million. All I'm after is to clear up the mess. This organization that seems to be operating under the name of the Golden Alligator has got me guessing. I'm in this thing not for the money but for the love of the fight—and I'm curious of course. The money itself adds zest to the case."

The Key shook his head.

"Believe me, you certainly are a honey of a guy to understand." He took a deep breath. "Well, anyway, I'm with you, kid. Where do we go from here?"

"You know where the Altoona hotel is?" King asked.

"Yeah. It's a second-rate dump in the east fifties. I've forgot just the exact number. What you going to do down there?"

"John Hernando," King explained, "said that he had taken down the names and addresses of the six men who applied in answer to this ad. Rather think that one of these men is responsible for the two murders that have been committed, and is connected with the organization known as the Golden Alligator. I want that list. Let's go."

"Is there anything you'd like to have us do while you're gone?" the Bishop asked.

King shook his head. "No. Just sit tight and listen for any news that may come from the Key's friends over the short-wave radio. I think we'll be back before evening, although I'm not sure."

King and the Key went from the cabin.

Luga followed King outside.

"Master," he said, "you not take me?"

"I'm afraid not this time, big boy. This isn't going to be a particularly dangerous job, I'm sure. But it might be if you went along and someone recognized you. Don't forget you stand out anywhere in a crowd."

"Yes, Master," said the big black. "Luga sorry sometimes."

"Yeah—but not other times," said King. "When it comes to fighting, that big figure of yours certainly comes in handy, Luga."

He and the Key strode on. They reached the place where the cars were hidden. King hesitated.

"I think," he said, "it would be a good idea if we took the roadster this time. That'll leave the sedan for the rest of them if they need it. Then, too, it might not be so good if that sedan was seen for a while."

"You mean you got in a jam with it?" the Key asked.

"Well, about as close as I ever hope to be without landing in jail," King laughed.

He kept on chuckling.

"I'll never forget that woman in the garage when I threw

stones up at her window. She thought I was her husband coming home drunk. There's one guy I feel kind of sorry for, in a way. But I suppose it's his own fault."

They climbed into the roadster. King was at the wheel. He backed out, turned into the secret bedrock driveway, and onto the main highway. Presently he turned west and to New York, a half-hour's drive.

They passed through the town where Katie Marshall ran the garage. King pointed it out to the Key. Then he ducked a little lower behind the side of the car. A police car was parked in front of the Marshall garage.

"Still looking for you," the Key observed.

"Yes," said King. "Wouldn't they be surprised if they knew I was in this roadster."

They drove on. Nearer New York the traffic grew heavier. They crossed over from Brooklyn and then proceeded uptown.

As they approached the fifties, the Key said, "Take it easy while I look down these streets at the signs. The Altoona is over east on one of these streets, but I can't remember which one."

King slowed while the Key examined the hotel signs on each one of the streets. They kept on until they came to 54th. Then they turned east. The Key stared.

"There she is," he said. "Right there on the left."

King pulled over, passing the entrance. He found a parking space a half a block or so below and they got out and walked back.

King, with the Key beside him, stepped to the desk.

"Mr. John Hernando is expecting me," King said. "Could you tell me his room number?"

The clerk scrutinized him and then ran down the file list of guests.

"Number 543," he said. "Do you want to call first?"

"No," King said. "We'll go right up."

He stepped into an elevator.

"Five," he told the operator. Then they were out in the hall on the fifth floor.

"This way," said the Key, leading him down the corridor.

Room 543 was in a dark part of the hall. King tried the door. It was locked, as he had expected. He stepped back and jerked his head toward it.

"Alright, Key, there's your job."

The Key grinned and produced a ring with several pieces of metal hanging on it. They were so small they could hardly be called skeleton keys. He glanced at the lock, selected a key, worked it for what seemed a little over a second. He turned the handle and pushed the door open.

KING ENTERED first. He stared about the room in astonishment. Apparently the bed hadn't been slept in but it was tumbled upside down and inside out. Even the mattress was slit open in places. He heard the Key chuckle.

"Looks like someone's been here ahead of us," he said.

"It would seem so," said King. "I hope they haven't got what I'm after."

The drawers of the dresser were pulled out and had been

ransacked. A suitcase stood on the low stand. Clothes were scattered about the place in wild disorder.

King went straight to the clothes closet and opened the door. He hesitated.

"I wonder," he said, "what these other birds were after."

"There's only one thing anybody would be after in a room with a guy that was hooked up with a hundred million dollars in gold," the Key ventured. "They'd be looking for a map or something that would show them where the buried treasure was."

King nodded.

"I hope so."

"What else would they be looking for?" demanded the Key.

"I'm hoping," said King, thrusting his hand in the inside pocket of a suit that hung on the rack, "that they aren't after the list of names of the men who applied in answer to Hernando's—"

He stopped for a moment. He was drawing his hand out of the pocket.

"Here's something. From the way these papers are stuffed back into the pocket they searched there too. They couldn't have been after that list, unless—"

Then he found an old envelope with the list Hernando had told him of.

"Hum," he said. "Well, here it is. With the six names. And one of these men is guilty—guilty of the murder of Hernando and Close."

The Key looked at the names over his shoulder. King read

them aloud. There were addresses and telephone numbers after each name.

"Frank Stanton," he read, "attorney. W.G. Fuller, financier. George M. Whitmore, M.D. That must be the doctor he spoke about. John L. Ogden, merchant. Anthony Robbins, banker. Clinton J. Freeman, headmaster.

"Well," King went on, "It looks as though the Secret 6 or at least part of them—are going to consult the six honest men.

"Clinton J. Freeman, headmaster. That must be the one who runs the boy's school on Long Island—and in Florida in the winter time—that Hernando mentioned. Evidently he was the most honest-looking character of the six, because he was the one that Hernando picked before he found his friend Close."

The Key looked bored. He shrugged.

"Well," he said, "now you've got the six names. What are you going to do with them? Go and ask them if they'd be interested in a nice little hot seat party for murdering a couple of guys?"

King smiled tolerantly.

"That's not such a bad idea, at that," he said. "I think I'll call them up."

"Oh. And ask them over the 'phone?" the Key grinned.

"No," said King. "I think I'll get them all down to a party here. I'll tell them I'm John Hernando and that we're all set to go. Then maybe I can think of some kind of a trick that will make the bird who's to blame for this speak out of turn. At any rate, it's worth trying."

He took a list with him and walked to the telephone. There he hesitated, turned to the Key, and glanced significantly at the list.

"I wonder," he said, "if this list of names was taken down as the men appeared? I don't suppose it would make any difference."

His eyes narrowed. He studied the list again.

"Still, it might have something to do with it," he said. "We'll keep it in mind."

"Don't ask me to keep anything in mind," said the Key. "Not when it gets to the stage of telling what kind of guy a bird is by his name."

King smiled.

"That's too much to ask of anyone," he said. "But that'll be something to remember. I'm going to assume from the start that these men did call in the order that they are put on the list. There is no reason to believe they didn't."

"Okay," said the Key. "Figure it out any way you like. It's far over my head already."

King glanced at his wrist watch.

"It's about time in the morning I ought to catch most of these men in—except possibly the doctor. We'll find out."

He got the operator and called the number of the first on the list, Frank Stanton, the attorney. The musical voice of a young woman answered.

"I'd like to speak to Mr. Stanton," said King.

"Who's calling, please?" she asked.

"Tell him John Hernando is calling from the Altoona Hotel. I think he'll understand."

"Yes, sir. Hold the line please."

Almost instantly the response came. It was a young alert voice that answered.

"Oh, Hernando. This is Frank Stanton speaking. I've been waiting to hear from you."

"Can you come over to the hotel in my room?" King asked.

"Gladly," said Stanton. "Immediately."

King hung up the receiver and called the next on the list, W.G. Fuller, who was rated as a financier.

AGAIN A young woman answered the 'phone.

"I'd like to speak to Mr. W. G. Fuller," he said.

"One moment," she replied. "I'll let you speak to his confidential secretary."

King took a long breath impatiently and waited. Then a very business-like woman's voice answered.

"Yes?"

"This is John Hernando speaking. I'd like to talk to Mr. W. G. Fuller, if possible."

"One moment. I'll see if he's in."

King winked at the Key. "She'll see if he's in. He'll be in alright."

Then he heard a sharp man's voice coming back over the wires to him.

"Mr. W.G. Fuller speaking. This you, Hernando?"

"Yes," said King. "I'd like to see you in my room here at the Altoona Hotel as soon as possible."

"About what we were discussing the other day?" Fuller asked.

"Yes."

"I'll be right over."

King hung up and called the next man, Dr. George M. Whitmore. A leisurely voice with a grate note answered this time.

"This is Dr. Whitmore."

"John Hernando speaking," said King. "You remember we were talking about that project in Florida, doctor?"

"Oh, yes. Yes, indeed," said the doctor.

"Could you come over to my room right away? I'd like to discuss it with you."

"By all means," said the doctor. "I have a call to make up in your section, anyway."

"Thank you," said King.

Next he called John L. Ogden, who was listed on the envelope as a merchant. A man's voice, rough and harsh answered rather sleepy. "Hello."

"Is this John L. Ogden?" King asked.

"No. Wait a minute."

Then King heard him at the side of the 'phone, calling.

"Hey, come here. Somebody wants to talk to you."

King's eyes narrowed.

"This doesn't sound like a mercantile establishment."

A rough, rasping voice answered at the other end.

"Hello. What's the matter?"

"Why, nothing that I know of," King said. "This is John Hernando at the Altoona Hotel. You remember we were talking over a little matter the other day?"

"Huh?" growled Ogden. "Say, wait a minute. What did you say?"

King nodded and winked at the Key.

"My name is John Hernando," he said. "You were over here the other day and we were discussing a project in Florida. Remember?"

"Oh, yeah. Sure. I'd almost forgotten. And you say you're Hernando?"

"Yes," said King. He hesitated a moment. "Is there any reason why I shouldn't be?"

"Why—why, no," said Ogden, as though he was taken by surprise. "No. Of course not," he growled. "Only reason I was surprised was because I thought the deal was off."

"It doesn't seem to be," said King. "I'd like to discuss it with you. Can you come over to my hotel?"

"Sure," answered the other. "I'll be right over."

"Fine."

He turned to the Key as he hung up.

"It begins to look as though we're getting somewhere," he said. "At least here's one man who doesn't fit into the picture. He sounds more like a thug to me."

The Key shook his head.

"Don't look at me," he said. "I didn't hear him talking."

King called Anthony Robbins, the next on the list. He was a banker. After making himself known to a young woman and later a young man, he was listening to an individual who admitted he was Anthony Robbins.

He had a quick way of saying things. There was a snap to his voice. And still there seemed to King to be a little weakness somewhere. Perhaps it gave him the feeling that the importance was mostly put-on.

"Yes," Robbins promised with eagerness. "I'll be right over. That's the Altoona Hotel, isn't it."

"Right," said King.

He called Clinton J. Freeman last. He was listed as the headmaster of a school. And when he was talking to him on the 'phone he realized why Hernando had chosen him from all the rest as a man to be trusted.

He spoke with perfect calm. His voice was that of a fatherly man with a kind, soft heart. Almost a little too soft, King guessed, to run a boy's preparatory school.

"Yes," Freeman promised. "It'll take me a little while to get in. But I'll meet you as soon as I can. You say this is Hernando?"

"Yes," said King.

Freeman hesitated.

"You're—at the Altoona Hotel?"

"Yes. The same place where we met before."

"Yes. Surely," said Freeman. "Very well, I'll be there as soon as I can."

They hung up.

King laughed as he turned to the Key again.

"Either the boys in Freeman's school love him too much to take advantage of him or else they have a whale of a good time."

"I wouldn't understand that, either," said the Key. "I don't remember much about any school I ever attended."

A knock sounded on the door. King stepped lightly to it and opened it quickly. A big, stern-looking man with a businesslike air stood in the hall. He stared at King.

"Is Hernando in?" he asked bluntly.

King nodded.

"Won't you step in?" he asked.

Never once did King take his eyes from that man's face. He stepped away and Fuller, the financier, came in. The big man looked about the room as King closed the door. Then he stared back at King again in surprise.

"Where is Hernando?" he demanded. King motioned him to a chair. He perched himself on a bed.

"The fact of the matter is, Mr. Fuller, Hernando is dead. I thought you might know something about it."

"Dead?" said the big man, without showing any great emotion. "That's odd. Why, I was talking to him only day before yesterday. Or was it yesterday?"

Then his face clouded.

"What the devil are you driving at? Why should I know anything about his death?" His eyes narrowed. "Say, come to think about it. Maybe I could throw a little light on it.

"I received a telephone call, and when I answered it, there was a man talking on the other end. He asked if I was W. G. Fuller and I told him I was. He said he understood I was interested in a project in Florida, and if I didn't want the Golden Alligator to get me I'd better forget about it."

King stiffened on the edge of the bed. His eyes were burning into the face of the other.

"Do you mind repeating that, Mr. Fuller?" he asked.

## CHAPTER 6
## SIX HONEST MEN

W.G. FULLER, brusk and business-like, shifted in the chair that he had taken. He took a cigar from his vest pocket, bit off the end and lighted it before complying with King's request.

"Let's see, I'll try to get it a little straighter as I tell it this time," he said.

"This telephone call came on the evening of the day that I was up here to see Hernando. I don't remember the exact time, but it was somewhere around the middle of the evening—perhaps 8 or 9 o'clock.

"I answered the 'phone myself. I heard a man's voice at the other end. I don't recall his exact words, but I remember the substance very well. He asked if I was W. G. Fuller, the financier, who was thinking of going into a project in Florida. I told him I was.

"Then he said, 'Forget it, if you don't want the Golden Alligator to get you.' I remember asking him what the Golden Alligator was but he had already hung up."

"What kind of a voice did he have?" asked King.

"A rather coarse, rasping voice, I'd say."

"Would you recognize it if you heard it again?"

"I'm quite sure I would."

"What did you do after you hung up?" King's next question came.

Fuller smiled.

"Well, to tell you the truth, I wasn't very deeply horrified by the threat. Not nearly as much as I am now. You see, I've never heard of anything called the Golden Alligator. As a matter of fact, I haven't the slightest idea now what it might be. I remember laughing at the idea afterwards."

"And that's all you did?" asked King with considerable surprise.

"Why, yes," said Fuller. "I'm afraid it is. What should I have done?"

"I don't know," said King. "But I should say off-hand that you might have notified the police."

Fuller shook his head.

"No," he said, "I hardly think so. Hernando explained that quite clearly right here in this room. And I can understand his viewpoint. The idea is that if the police know about this buried treasure the facts would be publicized very shortly. And those Ten Thousand Islands down off the coast of Florida would be filled with people from all over the United States looking for the buried treasure."

"But," King ventured, "didn't the warning frighten you?"

"No," said Fuller. "I haven't felt that I was in danger until now. As I hinted when I first mentioned it a few minutes ago, I rather took it as a joke. And it had almost slipped my mind until you told me of Hernando's death."

"But I can't understand that. You must have realized something queer was going on. People as a rule don't get secret warnings over the telephone and then just forget them."

"Not ordinarily," went on Fuller, "but I had dinner at my club that evening and mentioned the proposition rather vaguely to three or four friends while I was eating.

"Some of the boys are great on playing pranks. So when I received the telephone call I simply figured that they had cooked up this thing for a little joke."

"Did you tell them that the gold was supposed to be buried in the Ten Thousand Islands?" King asked.

"No," said Fuller. "I simply said that the gold was supposed to be buried somewhere around Florida, and one invariably associates Florida with alligators, of course.

"And the combination of the gold and the alligators would make them think of the gold alligator or something of that kind. I didn't want to let them think I was frightened by the affair, so I carried on without saying any more about it—just as though I knew all the time it was a little joke of theirs.

"But now—" He moved a little nervously. "From what you've told me it seems to be quite a serious matter."

King nodded.

"I can certainly assure you it is, Mr. Fuller." He hesitated. "You say, Mr. Fuller, you're quite sure you'd recognize the voice if you heard it again?"

"Yes. I'm quite sure. On the other hand, now that I think of it, it sounded to me as though the voice was disguised. I believe that's one thing that made me believe it was some friend at the club playing a joke on me."

"But you might recognize it if you heard it again, even though it was disguised?"

"Perhaps not," said Fuller. "But I'd be glad to try."

"You'll have an opportunity—at least I expect you will," King observed.

The financier looked perplexed.

"You mean here?"

King nodded.

"Do you know how many answered the advertisement of John Hernando for an honest man?" he asked.

**FULLER SHOOK** his head.

"I met four of them out in the hall. We all came about the same time. And Hernando admitted us one by one and talked to each of us in here alone."

"Do you remember who they were?"

"Their names?" asked Fuller.

"Yes," said King.

"I'm sorry but I don't remember any of them. I'd know them if I saw them again, of course."

"I hope you'll have that opportunity. The fact remains that there were six altogether, including yourself. You met four. That, with you, makes five. Will you do this to help me, Mr. Fuller?"

"Anything that I can," he replied.

"Will you," King asked, "as each comes in, nod to tell me whether you met him in the hall outside or not?"

"Gladly," said Fuller.

A knock sounded at the door.

"There's someone now," said King. "After they come in you watch me. I'll glance that way. If you met them out in the hall you nod your head in the affirmative, slightly. If you didn't meet them, shake your head in the negative. I'll understand."

"Very well," said Fuller.

King got up and walked to the door. A young man of leisurely manner stood outside. He was slightly stooped. The suit that he wore was badly in need of pressing. His necktie was not straight at the front of his collar. Altogether, his general appearance was shabby.

He glanced at King. "Is Mr. Hernando in?"

"Won't you come in?" said King. "This is the right place."

The young man nodded and entered. He looked at the Key and Fuller. The financier bowed.

King glanced at Fuller who nodded very slightly.

"I believe I met you up here day before yesterday, didn't I?" the young man asked Fuller.

"Yes—out in the hall where we were all waiting."

The young man turned questioningly to King.

"I don't see Mr. Hernando anywhere."

By now King had closed the door.

"I'm afraid," he said, "you won't. Do you mind telling me your name?"

"Stanton—Frank Stanton. I'm an attorney."

"Oh, yes," said King. "You're the first on the list."

"On what list?" asked Stanton.

"On the list John Hernando left."

"But I understood that Hernando was going to be here."

"I'm afraid," said King, "it was necessary for me to trick you into thinking he was. But you're not alone in that, Mr. Stanton. You see Hernando was murdered early this morning. That's one of the main reasons I'm bringing all you gentlemen together.

I've a very strong feeling that one of you men who answered the advertisement is responsible for Hernando's death."

"Am I to understand," asked Stanton, "That I'm being questioned by the police?"

King smiled and shook his head.

"No. As a matter of fact, it's quite the contrary. I'll try to explain everything a little more fully after everyone is here."

Another knock sounded at the door. King opened it.

A medium-sized, well-dressed man with a close-cut gray mustache stood at the door.

"I'm Dr. Whitmore—Dr. George M. Whitmore," he said. "Is Mr. Hernando in? I believe this is the right room."

"Yes, Dr. Whitmore, this is the right room, but John Hernando won't be here with us. He was murdered last night."

Whitmore's mouth dropped open.

"Murdered?" he gasped.

Then King thought he assumed a professional air instantly.

"Where did this happen?"

"I will tell you all about it shortly if you'll be patient. That's what I called you gentlemen here for."

He shot a glance at Fuller, the financier. Fuller gave a short nod.

Both of these men had been here with Fuller before.

"While I think of it," King said, his eyes still leveled on Fuller's face, "you say, Mr. Fuller, you didn't know the names of any of the other men?"

"No," said Fuller. "They were all strangers to me when I met them out in the hall."

King turned to the doctor who had just entered.

"You remember meeting Mr. Fuller outside day before yesterday?"

"Yes," said the doctor. "The three of us and two others were out there for a few moments together. Then Hernando asked me to come in first as I was the first one to arrive. It seems a very strange coincidence, all five of us coming up in the same elevator. It just so happened that we got here at the same time."

"There was no one else in this room with Hernando when you arrived?"

"No," said the doctor.

King glanced at the financier.

"No," Fuller said. "No, I'm sure there wasn't. Not unless there was someone else hiding under the bed."

KING GLANCED under the bed instinctively.

"It would be rather hard," he said, "to hide under that bed without any one of you seeing him. There was no mention of names or addresses or telephone numbers among you gentlemen?"

"None that I remember," said Fuller. The other two shook their heads in negative. The rather unkempt young attorney shifted nervously.

"A very strange thing happened to me night before last," he said. "I've been trying to figure out what to do about it ever since. I didn't report it to the police because Hernando expressed a wish that this—er—affair be kept strictly private.

"I was working at the office night before last when a telephone call came. A man with a rather harsh voice asked if I was the Frank Stanton who was considering a proposition in Florida. When I partially admitted that I was he said, 'forget it if you don't want the Golden Alligator to kill you!'"

King shot a glance at the financier. Saw him puffing rapidly on his cigar. Then, just as he swung his eyes to the doctor, Dr. Whitmore spoke.

"That's a strange coincidence," he said. "You say that was night before last, Mr. Stanton?"

Stanton nodded.

"About what time did you say?" the doctor asked.

"A quarter of nine. I glanced at my watch and checked the time. Then I called back and had the operator locate the place where the call had come from. It was a pay station in Brooklyn."

"And you didn't report it to the police?" King asked the attorney.

"No," he replied.

King happened to glance back at the face of the doctor. It had a ruddy hue, shading off to almost white toward his ears. The doctor coughed twice.

"Very peculiar," he said. "It may sound fantastic, but I had a similar thing happen to me on the same evening. My call came a few minutes after nine. I, too, checked the source of the call and found that it came from a pay station in Brooklyn. Just as Mr. Stanton has stated."

King turned to the financier.

"You say, Mr. Fuller, you didn't have the call checked?"

"No," said Fuller. "Of course not. As I explained before I

supposed the call came from one of my club associates as a joke, so I didn't pay much attention to it."

King turned back to Dr. Whitmore.

"What did you do about it, doctor?"

"Aside from a great deal of very serious thinking I haven't done anything about it."

*Knock! Knock! Knock!*

King leaped for the door and swung it open. Glanced at the slim, dapper man outside.

"I'm Mr. Robbins. Is Mr. Hernando in?" he asked.

King stepped aside.

"Won't you come in, Mr. Robbins?"

He remembered the list of names. Closed the door.

"You're Anthony Robbins?" he said. "You're listed as a banker?"

"Yes," said Mr. Robbins, rather nervously, glancing about. "Yes, that's right."

King glanced at Fuller. Received a nod. This was another one of the five who had met before.

The banker hesitated. Half turned toward the door.

"Perhaps there is some mistake here. I understood that Mr. Hernando wanted to see me privately."

"That must be a mistaken idea," said King. "I called in place of Mr. Hernando."

Robbins frowned.

"But I understood the person I talked to over the 'phone to say that he was Hernando, himself."

King smiled very slightly.

"I'm afraid I took upon myself to lie a little bit about the situation," he said. "You see, Hernando is dead."

"Dead!" the banker yelled.

"He was murdered last night or, I should say, early this morning. That's why I called you gentlemen in on the case. There are two more to hear from. I thought perhaps one of you might throw a little light on the subject."

"And who are you?" demanded Robbins.

"For the time being," King answered, "you can list me in your mental directory as a detective. I believe my present occupation will certainly fill that category."

He glanced about at the others. Then swung back quickly to face Robbins.

"Robbins," he snapped, "has anything happened in connection with this case since you visited John Hernando here day before yesterday?"

Robbins hesitated. Glanced rather nervously about at the others.

"Am I to assume," he demanded, "that I'm being suspected in a criminal light in this case?"

KING ANSWERED indirectly.

"Until this case is cleared up, Robbins," he said, "practically everyone is suspected of being connected with the murder. But, of course, if you're an innocent man you'll take every opportunity to tell what you know."

A frightened look crossed Robbins' face for a moment.

"Yes, of course," he nodded.

"There was something rather peculiar that has happened in

connection with this case since you left this room day before yesterday?" King probed.

Robbins nodded.

"Great Scott!" cried Dr. Whitmore. "Don't tell me you we're—"

"Wait," snapped King. "I'll handle the questioning. Mr. Robbins doesn't need any help from anyone else." His eyes were level on Robbins.

"Yes," Robbins said, like a man eager to get something off his mind. "Something did happen after I left here. I haven't been able to figure it out since."

"And what was it?" King asked.

"A telephone call," said Robbins. "A man with a gruff voice called. I can't remember the exact words, because none of it made much sense, except that the caller stated very bluntly that I'd better forget anything about a Florida project. There was something about being threatened with a golden alligator. He hung up after that."

King nodded to the rest and took a long breath.

"Well," he said, "that makes four. Perhaps we'll find one out of the six who didn't receive this call regarding the Golden Alligator."

Another knock came. King answered the door as before.

This man was large. He had a heavy jaw. A cigar clenched between his teeth. He was a powerful, hard-looking individual. There was no uncertainty about stating his name or what he came for.

"I'm John L. Ogden," he said in a deep voice. "I came to see Hernando. He called me. Where is he?"

"Come in, Mr. Ogden," King said. And he couldn't help feeling that the "John L" fitted him quite well. The man looked strikingly like a former pugilist. Ogden stepped inside. There was an atmosphere of calm assurance about him.

"You know these other men?" King asked.

Ogden nodded to Stanton, Fuller, Whitmore and Robbins.

"I've seen those four before—met them out in the hall day before yesterday."

King glanced at Fuller, who nodded.

Ogden glanced at the Key who was sitting over in a corner, half slumped in his chair.

"I've seen him before," Ogden said. "But I can't remember just where."

King glanced at the list of names in his hand.

"You're listed as a merchant, Mr. Ogden. Is that right?"

"Huh?" said Ogden. "Oh. A merchant. Yeah. That's right."

King stared hard at him. Somehow, Ogden didn't look like any merchant he'd ever seen before. He wasn't the merchant type.

"I thought Hernando was here?" Ogden said.

"I'm afraid," said King, "I lied a little about that. Hernando won't ever be here again."

"No?" said Ogden. "Why not?"

"I rather hoped that you could answer that," said King.

"Me?" asked Ogden. "Why should I know anything about him? I haven't seen him since we met here day before yesterday."

King's eyes were narrowed on him. Probing for the secret that it seemed this man must have. His very appearance seemed to accuse him.

"Say, what's all this about, anyway?" he demanded suddenly.

Instead of answering that directly, King said, "Try to remember what happened since you left Hernando here day before yesterday. You met these other four men here at the same time. Is that right?"

"Yes," growled Ogden.

"Has anything happened in connection with Hernando since that time?"

Ogden shook his head.

"Not that I know of—say, who are you, anyway?"

King smiled slowly.

"For the time being," he said, "you can consider me a detective in the case."

"Oh, yeah?"

"Yeah," said King. And the smile left his face.

A sixth knock sounded on the door.

A tall man, perhaps fifty, stood there as King opened it. His eyes were dark and his hair was quite black. He smiled as he looked at King. A radiant, kind, fatherly smile.

"I came in answer to a call from Hernando," he said.

"Yes," said King. "You must be—"

"Freeman," cut in the other, his genial smile broadening.

"Oh, yes. Mr. Freeman. Clinton J. Freeman," King went on. "You're headmaster of a school on Long Island with winter headquarters in Florida. That correct?"

He stepped aside and Freeman came in. "Yes. Yes, indeed," he replied.

THEN HE glanced at the others and a look of perplexity crossed his brow.

"But who are these? I don't believe I've had the pleasure of—"

King closed the door. He glanced at Fuller. The financier shook his head. This man wasn't one of the five he had met out in the hall.

King faced him.

"I believe," he said, "Mr. Freeman, you answered an ad in a paper a couple of days ago?"

"Yes. That's correct. It was an advertisement for an honest man to finance some kind of a buried treasure project in Florida."

"If I have the story right," King said, "you were chosen as the most honest-appearing of these six who answered the ad. You were picked to finance the proposition by John Hernando in preference to the others."

"Yes. I was ready and willing to go into the proposition."

"But Hernando changed his mind," King went on, "because after he met you he found the man whom he originally came to New York to see."

"That is correct," said Freeman. "At least that's what Mr. Hernando told me. Of course, since he found someone whom he preferred to go into the matter with him, I naturally—er—stepped out of the picture, as you might say."

King's eyes shifted from the hard-looking Ogden to the gentle schoolmaster of a boy's school.

"John Hernando," he said, "was murdered last night."

"Murdered?" gasped Freeman. "Why—it doesn't seem possible. I can hardly believe it."

"But before he died," King went on savagely, "he told me the whole story. Some of the others here have told me what they knew. I've called all six of you together to see if someone couldn't throw some light on the situation.

"Can you, Mr. Freeman, tell us anything bearing on this matter?"

Freeman frowned and dropped his eyes to the carpet on the floor.

"Yes," he said slowly. "I can. There was a telephone call that I received. I don't remember the exact time. I might say it was somewhere between 9 and 10 o'clock.

"I can't recall ever having heard the voice before. It was a man. He warned me against going into this proposition. There was some mention of the Golden Alligator.

"I've done a great deal of thinking about it since. As a matter of fact, I've been very grateful that Hernando changed his mind and wished to have someone else see him through the proposition."

"Why?" demanded King.

Freeman hesitated—seemed at a loss where to begin for a moment.

"Have you ever," he asked, "studied the subject of buried treasure?"

"No," said King.

"Well, then, perhaps you wouldn't know," Freeman went on.

"But that study has been more or less a hobby with me. Ever since I read *Treasure Island* as a boy it's had a sort of fascination for me. I presume a great many men have such hobbies in one form or another.

"And because of my study of the subject I was particularly glad that Mr. Hernando had chosen someone beside me to see the thing through. That is, after I received the telephone call. You see, there is such a thing as the Golden Alligator!"

John L. Ogden glared at him.

"What are you talking about?" he said. "You mean there is a Golden Alligator. Something like a goldfish?"

"No, indeed," said Freeman tolerantly. "It's about as far removed from a fish as anything could be. The Golden Alligator is the name of an organization that was formed by a half-brother of Captain Kidd. It was instrumental in sending Captain Kidd to the gallows. And the organization, which I understand still exists, has as its aim the finding of Captain Kidd's enormous treasure."

"I've understood," said Doctor Whitmore, "that some of Captain Kidd's treasure formed the basis of the Van Ripkin fortune."

Freeman smiled at the doctor as a headmaster to a small boy.

"That's partly true," he agreed. "But it was a very small percentage of Captain Kidd's buried treasure. The larger bulk is still buried. That is the gold that our late friend, John Hernando, was connected with."

The shabbily dressed attorney leaned forward.

"Why," he asked, "would this organization be known as the Golden Alligator?"

"It seems very simple," said Freeman. "When you understand that the chest, in which the gold was buried had a gold plate with some strange figures upon it.

"And, in addition, it had a golden alligator. That is, a small alligator made of solid gold mounted on a plate as though it were crawling.

"It is the belief of this organization, who are probably descendants of Captain Kidd's half-brother, that the code lettering on the plate of this chest directs anyone, who knows enough to read it, to the hiding place of the main body of the treasure. That, from what Hernando said, was something in the neighborhood of a hundred million."

He glanced at the others.

"That's what Hernando told you, is it not?"

They all nodded.

King's eyes narrowed. He had been standing all the time in front of the door. The only door in the room. Now he let his gaze fall upon John L. Ogden.

"Mr. Ogden," he said, "I think we'd like to have you answer a few questions. Where were you night before last between 9:30 and 10 o'clock?"

Ogden's face went purple with rage.

"That's none of your damn business!" he flared. "Besides, I don't remember."

He took a step toward King. King stood his ground.

## CHAPTER 7
## IN THE HANDS OF THE LAW

"WHAT I want to know," John L. Ogden roared, "is who you think you are?"

King thought Ogden was coming straight for him, but he never wavered.

"It seems enough for you to know now," said King, "that I'm handling the investigation in this case. And you might be very interested to know that I'm looking directly in the face of the man that I think is responsible for the two murders last night."

"What two murders?" demanded Ogden.

"Yes," Freeman said, "I'm sure we'd all be very much interested to know who besides John Hernando was murdered."

"Very well," said King. "I'll tell you."

He was still standing in front of the door but he was looking at Freeman.

"You recall, Mr. Freeman," he said, "that Hernando decided to have a man by the name of Close, that architect friend of his, finance the project after he learned his whereabouts. That, I believe, is the main reason he decided against you."

"That's correct," said Freeman. "But don't tell me Close was murdered?"

"I'm afraid I'll have to," said King. "I was eating breakfast on the paved terrace with him this morning when he was killed by a flying garrote exactly like the one that killed Hernando."

Then King took one of the strange weapons from his pocket and held it up so everyone could see.

"And, gentlemen," he said, "there is what I refer to as a flying garrote."

"Huh?" said Ogden, staring at it. "How does it work?"

"Your acting is very good, Ogden," smiled King. "But not quite good enough.

"It seems the Senegalese used them sometime ago. I believe it's against the law now in French Senegal. They hold one of the weights and twirl it around their head, letting the weight at the other end fly. Then, whirling it in that fashion, they throw it at their victim.

"A good marksman, I'm told, can make a killing at quite a distance. The neck or throat of the individual is the part aimed at. When the wire strikes, the weights fly round his neck in opposite directions. The wire winds very tightly and chokes him to death almost instantly."

Ogden held out his hand for the flying garrote. But King drew it back.

"Ogden," he said, "it looks very much to me as though you're the man I want. You're sure nothing happened in reference to this case since you saw Hernando day before yesterday?"

Ogden flushed.

"Certainly not," he said. "Nothing that I know of."

He hesitated a moment.

"Say," he said, "maybe there was something. I got back to my office night before last. I guess it was around 11 or 12 o'clock and my—er—secretary told me that somebody had called three or four times. I wasn't in."

"The person who called didn't leave any message, did he?"

"No," said Ogden. "I don't remember anything about it."

"Very well," said King. "You'll all pardon me a moment while I speak to my assistant. Then I think you may all go."

He shot a glance at the Key sitting over in the corner. Jerked his head to him. The Key got up and came over. King opened the door and ushered him out into the hall. Then he stepped after him and closed the door.

When they were alone, King said, "Key, what do you think of this?"

He shrugged.

"I wouldn't trust that guy Ogden any farther than I could throw a safe."

"It's hard to tell," said King.

The Key stared at him in the dark hallway. "You don't mean you're going to let him walk off? Why, that guy is as guilty as they make them."

"Perhaps," said King. "But we've got to be sure. Here's what I want you to do. I'm going to send all six of these men home or wherever they want to go.

"I want you to hop on Ogden's tail and shadow him. See where he goes. I'll wait here in the hotel room for you. Don't let him know he's being shadowed."

"Trust me," grinned the Key.

"I do," said King. "Now go downstairs and hang around the lobby until he comes down. Then follow him."

"Okay," said the Key.

King went back into the room. The Key was walking toward the elevator.

"Gentlemen," King said, "I have talked it over with my assistant. We have come to the conclusion that I'm wrong. I'm going to permit all of you to go your way. I'm afraid I'll have to look elsewhere for the guilty party."

He opened the door and bowed them out one by one. They all seemed glad to leave.

ALL EXCEPT Freeman. He was last. And he bowed to King.

"This is certainly a most interesting case," he said. "You can appreciate my feeling regarding it since I've made such a hobby of buried treasure study. It's most interesting, I can assure you. If there is anything I can do don't fail to call on me. Here's my card."

"Thank you," said King as he took the card. Then Freeman was gone and King closed the door.

"There's one sure thing in my mind," he said to himself. "Ogden's no more of a merchant than I am. On the other hand there's some of the rest of those men whom I haven't too much faith in when it comes to a hundred million dollars.

"Take, for instance, the first one that came—Fuller. I'll bet he drives a hard bargain. I'd hate to have my life hanging in the balance with him with a hundred million at stake. I hope the Key will call me as soon as he finds where Ogden's trail leads."

Several minutes passed. He stood staring out of the window when he heard the sound of footsteps on the carpeted hall. He turned toward the door.

There was no knock. The door was thrown open abruptly and four of the New York police walked in.

The sergeant in charge said in a gruff voice:

"No monkey business now. You're under arrest."

King nodded.

"I might have guessed this," he said. "I'd like to know who called up and turned me in."

"So would we," said the sergeant. "But I guess we've got the right man. I've seen you before somewhere."

"So have I," said another one of the officers. "We'll figure out where before we get through with you."

"Do you mind," King asked, "telling me just what this is all about? Just why am I under arrest?"

"You're under arrest," said the sergeant, "for murder. For the murder of Close, the architect, out on Long Island this morning."

"That's fine," said King.

"Huh?" said the sergeant, staring at him.

King smiled a little.

"I said that's fine. I'm working on a case that involves Close's death and the murder of another. I'm positive now that the man behind those murders was one of the six men who left here not over five minutes ago. I think I know which one it is, too. I'll know as soon as I—"

He stopped short.

"That's right. I'm under arrest. In that case, I probably won't get a chance to talk to the party I was thinking of."

"You'll get a chance to talk plenty when you get to police headquarters. Come on now. And no foolishness or we'll drill you."

While the sergeant kept his revolver leveled on him, one of

the other police officers stepped behind him. His hands flashed over King's body with an expert move.

"He's got nothing on him," the cop said. "Except—hey, what's this?"

He dipped his hand in King's pocket and took out the one flying garrote that he carried. Held it up and stared at it curiously. The other cops gathered round to add their questioning stares.

"What is it?" demanded the sergeant.

"You certainly ought to know," King said. "You've arrested me for the murder of Close. That happens to be the thing he was murdered with."

"What are you talking about?" the sergeant bawled.

"That's absolutely true," said King. "I was having breakfast with him at his château when it happened."

"How does it work?" asked the sergeant.

King smiled.

"Apparently you've never encountered this form of death in the United States."

King explained how the weapon worked and told of its origin.

"What are these gold lizards doing on each end of this wire?" asked one of the cops.

"Those don't happen to be lizards," King said. "Not unless you're speaking generally of the family. Those are golden alligators."

"You seem to know quite a lot about it," said the sergeant.

"I ought to," said King. "It seems to be general history. That is, the Golden Alligator part of it. And it so happened that I was with both men who were murdered with this weapon this morning. You probably don't know anything about the other one."

"Well, you know enough to be worth taking down to headquarters," said the sergeant. "So come along."

"Okay. I guess there isn't anything I can do about it. The sooner we get this over with the better satisfied I'll be."

As they walked down the hall to the elevator, King thought he caught a glimpse of a figure in the shadows at the end of the hall—a figure that might be watching. He wasn't sure.

A police car was in front of the hotel. He was placed between two of the burly cops and they drove off to headquarters.

The sergeant took him in before the captain.

The captain glanced at the sergeant.

"What's the charge?" he asked.

"Murder," said the sergeant. "This is the guy that somebody called up about in room 543 in the Altoona Hotel."

"Oh, yes," said the captain. "So you're the one that murdered Close, the architect, this morning, eh?"

"And here's what we found in one of his pockets," the sergeant said, producing the flying garrote. "He admits what it's used for too."

The captain's eyes narrowed.

"Well, what have you got to say for yourself, young man? What's your name?"

"I don't believe," King said, "it would do any good if I told you my name."

Suddenly the sergeant who had brought him blurted out:

"Say! Wait a minute! I think I got it. Isn't this the guy that escaped from the deathhouse several months ago?"

THE CAPTAIN stared harder. "It looks like him," he said.

"If it is," the sergeant went on, "you know who we got here, don't you?"

The captain grinned.

"Is there anybody on the force who wouldn't? Here we spend half our time chasing this Secret 6 gang and here you birds bring in the leader just like he was an ordinary panhandler without a license."

King smiled.

"If you mean that you think I'm King of the Secret 6, which I judge is the case from your conversation, I'm certainly highly flattered."

"Yeah?" said the captain. "Well, don't forget we're tickled to death to have you as a guest here. There isn't anybody that the boys could have picked up anywhere that they would like any better than you."

"Provided," King said, "that I'm the person you think I am."

"There ain't any doubt about that," said the captain. "Hey, Michaels, get out the fingerprint records of the fellow that was booked as King. You know—the one that escaped from the deathhouse."

"Yes, sir," called Michaels. "I'll have them there in a minute."

Then he came with the identification card, fingerprints, three-view photos and full description.

The captain took them, looked at the pictures. Compared them with King's face.

"It's the same guy," he said. "But just so you won't have any argument we'll check up your fingerprints."

He shoved forward an ink pad. The sergeant pressed King's finger-tips on it, and transferred them to paper. The captain compared the originals with the ones newly made.

A troubled look came into his eyes. He couldn't know that the Doctor had performed a clever operation on both the Key's and King's finger-tips so that they couldn't be successfully compared.

King laughed suddenly.

"What's the trouble? Don't they match, captain?"

The captain glared at him. "Alright," he said. "Maybe there's something funny about this. But you're not going to get off this easy."

"The funny part of it is," King said, "that twice in the last two months I've been suspected of being this person you call King of the Secret 6. It's very flattering, I'll admit. But it's very annoying, too. It seems to be my hard luck that I was born to look like this fellow King. Both times the fingerprints have been compared they've seen the difference of course."

"Yeah?" drawled the captain. "But don't forget that those other times you weren't arrested for murder like you are now. It sort of looks like you're on your own now—you can't blame this jam on the Secret 6."

He jerked his head toward the sergeant.

"Take him out back and lock him up. We'll save him. And the rest of you boys go off and learn more about this proposition so we'll have something definite to go on."

The sergeant took King by the arm. King was thinking as

rapidly as he could under the circumstances. But there seemed no way out for the present. He heard the click of the locking bar at the cell door.

The sergeant turned and grinned at him.

"You'll keep," he said.

After he had clumped off down the corridor, King walked about his cell, inspecting the interior. It was typical of many—a heavily barred opening for a window, steel sides, a cot that let down with chains and bare plumbing fixtures.

After that one tour of inspection he sat down on a bunk. Took a cigarette out of his pocket and lighted it. They had taken the flying garrotes away from him and placed them on the captain's desk.

In his mind he reviewed the happenings of the day.

Somehow he could no longer believe that the actual murderer had been one of the six he had seen in the hotel room.

None of those six men looked as though he had spent enough time in Africa to learn to handle the flying garrote with such unerring precision.

A jail attendant brought in the evening meal. He had missed lunch altogether. King took a few coins from his pocket. "Is there a chance to buy cigarettes here?" he asked. "I've smoked all I had."

The jail attendant grinned. "Feeling kind of nervous?"

"No, I'm just trying to think some things out. I do them better while I'm smoking."

The guard took the change and pushed the tray of food through a slot in the door.

"What kind do you want?" he asked. King named his favorite brand and the guard turned away without a word.

Later when he came back to get the empty tray he brought two packs of cigarettes and matches. He stared curiously at King.

"So you're the guy that's at the head of the Secret 6?" he asked.

"What do you think?" asked King, forcing a smile.

"I think I'd rather be in my shoes than in yours," said the other.

King laughed. "I do seem to be in pretty much of a jam, don't I? What's the next move?"

The other shrugged.

"Third degree, I suppose," he said.

"More than likely," said King. But he didn't feel so cheerful about that third degree as he acted. Brutal affair, that.

After the guard had taken the tray he sat and smoked. It grew dark and dim lights shone in the corridors. He was thinking about other things now. Thinking about getting out—trying to map out a course of action when he did get out—if ever.

It would be hard to pin that death sentence on him with the finger-prints that didn't check. On the other hand, strange things happen in legal circles at times.

He wondered if the Dummy had heard of his trouble. And if he had relayed the news from the police headquarters to the Secret 6 hide-out by short wave radio.

And he wondered, too, if the rest of the Secret 6 had learned of his trouble, how they would go about getting him out. He had no doubt but that they would make the attempt.

As he sat there with nothing else to do, his mind turned again to the case of the Golden Alligator. If he could only get a report from the Key he might know more.

"I suppose he followed Ogden," he said half aloud, "and knows all about him by this time. But that isn't going to do me any good as long as I'm in here."

He laid back on the cot dejectedly. Stared up at the darkened ceiling of steel.

Suddenly he jerked upright to a sitting position. Then he was standing, pressing against the door.

A sound had come to him from down the corridor that had snapped him out of his revery!

## CHAPTER 8
## THE GOLDEN ALLIGATOR

A S KING listened the sounds of a veritable riot came to him. There was shouting and yelling and howls of pain. Then the roar of a deep, bellowing voice like the roar of a bullet.

*Crash! Bam! Crack!*

Things seemed to be going wild out there. There were thudding sounds and three times there came the bark of a gun.

Then came the rapid thudding of light feet as a man was running down the corridor between the cells.

A choking voice at the other end of the corridor shouted, "Stop that black—"

Then it died away in a gurgling sound as though the speaker had been suddenly seized by a choking spasm.

The sound of the running feet came nearer.

*Bam!*

A gun bellowed in the hall. And the dim light that was nearest the cell popped and went out. King was straining against the grating of his door—straining to look down the corridor to see who might be coming and what all the commotion was about.

Then the door gave way before him as he leaned against it. The great long bar system that locked all the doors had been drawn back!

He half fell and half leaped out in the corridor between the cells. He saw other doors swing open, heard several prisoners cry out in astonishment.

Then a huge figure lunged down the passageway between the barred cells.

There was something familiar about that man—the way he moved—and his blackness. King couldn't see his face clearly. It was too dark.

"Luga!" he hissed.

Before he could say more he was picked up bodily, like a rag doll, and thrown over the shoulder of the giant black.

Then the negro whirled around and headed back the way he had come. He reached an open door, swerved and stooped so that his head and King's body wouldn't touch the top casing.

King stared about in the wake of the running man as he was being carried. A sight of horror met his gaze. Police officers seemed to be lying everywhere. There was one lying in a pool of blood. The captain was slumped over his desk, a revolver in his hand.

"Luga!" barked King. "What's the meaning of this? I've told you never to kill a policeman. I—"

Suddenly King felt himself whirled through the air. He was being jammed through a car door. His head hit the top. Stars blinked out before him.

He struggled to regain consciousness.

Something was wrong here. Something very wrong. This didn't seem at all like a rescue that the Secret 6 would put on. Things were getting dimmer and dimmer.

Then something was tied with brutal force over his mouth. He thought he could hear the grumbling of a motor. Thought he could feel the car rushing into action.

But he couldn't be sure of anything. He was gradually getting less and less conscious. Then everything seemed to fade entirely as a heavy cloth went over his head and smothered him.

His hands had been thrust behind him and kinked up behind his back until they hurt.

Then there was no more hurt—no more sensibility. He lapsed into oblivion.

When he regained consciousness he was being carried— apparently by one person.

He tried to hear what was going on about him. But the heavy cloth muffled his ears.

He had no idea of what direction they had taken after they left the police station. They might have driven in that car for ten minutes or ten hours.

Very faintly he heard a door close. As yet not a word of conversation came to him. It was a well-planned escape or kidnaping.

Surely, by now, if his getting away had been engineered by the Secret 6, he would have been told of it.

He struggled to get his arms free, but he was as powerless as a babe in arms.

Then he was being hurled from the shoulders of the man who was carrying him and felt himself dropped unceremoniously to the ground. Or was it a floor? It felt like heavy, creaking boards.

Still no other sounds.

Someone was fumbling with his hands that were tied behind his back and his arms were jerked against something. And he realized he was leaning against a post. A big round, vertical timber of some kind.

The tightening motion on the thongs that bound his wrists stopped. And the cloth vanished as though by magic from his eyes.

He turned his head to learn who had been doing all this. Received a vicious slap on the side of his face that sent his brain reeling.

He blinked in the dim light. Gradually his eyes became more accustomed to it. Was he in a room? He couldn't tell. A glow of light came from behind him. And he saw something step out of the shadows.

The dark giant form of a negro. The negro that he had taken to be Luga. But this negro was even larger than Luga. Had a ugly face. And where Luga's hair was wild and flying in all directions, the hair of this negro was short and kinky. The black man was dressed in a business suit with large shoes on his flat feet.

HE TURNED and stared down at King. "You ought to be glad I got you out of jail," he said.

"I might," King said, "if you hadn't killed all those cops in doing it."

"What do you care?" retorted the giant black. "You got any

King stared about from the shoulders of his rescuer. The police court was a shambles.

love for cops? You're King of the Secret 6, ain't you? That's what the cops said you were."

"How do you know?" demanded King.

The negro laughed.

"Oh, I got ways of knowing everything," he said. "You think you and your Secret 6 know everything. Well, I'm the fella that knows just a little bit more than you do."

King's eyes narrowed.

"Say," he demanded, "Who's behind all this?"

The negro laughed again.

"I'm pretty much on my own."

Then he added quickly, with a furtive glance behind him in the darker shadows.

"But if I was doing this for somebody else I wouldn't tell you who he was."

"Where did you learn to throw the flying garrote?" King demanded.

The negro chuckled.

"My grandpappy taught me to throw that when I was a little tiny fella. He tole me it might come in handy some day. And it sure has."

"I can imagine," said King, "you get pretty good money out of this."

"Yes," he said. "That's what it comes in handy for."

Then his expression suddenly changed.

"Say. Who the debble says I'm getting paid for this?"

King laughed now.

"I'm just using common sense," he said. "I know mighty well

that a big black like you wouldn't have sense enough to work all this stuff out. And I know, too, that Captain Kidd's half-brother wasn't a black man."

The negro strode toward him menacingly. For a moment it looked as though he was going to raise one of those giant feet and kick King full in the face.

"What you talking 'bout, man?" he demanded.

"You know," said King. "The Golden Alligator."

The negro grinned again.

"You want to see the gold alligator? Believe me, you're going to see him soon enough without hurrying things."

"I'd like to very much," said King.

"After you see him and he get you, you'll wish you hadn't seen him," said the colored man. "What I want to know, what's you and your Secret 6 messing around in something that ain't you business for?"

"That," said King, "is our business and not yours."

The other shrugged.

"Alright, white man," he said. "But you're going to find out before you get through that you can't mess with me. You want to see the gold alligator? Alright, you just hold on. You'll see him in less than five minutes!"

He pointed across the great room now. King stared in that direction. And he began to get his bearings for the first time.

Outside somewhere he heard a throbbing sound like an engine puffing along. And his nostrils, that had been so choked up with the musty, dirty odor of the heavy cloth, detected the fishy smell of the wharves.

He saw a low, wide door at the side of the room. Then he decided he was somewhere down among the docks, either on the East River or the Hudson River side of Manhattan.

No, he wasn't in either of those places. Those telephone calls of warning had come from some pay stations in Brooklyn. If this tallied with that, he was probably in one of those lower wharves on the Brooklyn side of the East River.

He stared harder at the door that the giant negro was striding toward. King marveled at the lightness of his tread on the heavy floor. The black man stopped beside the door and laughed again.

"So," he said, "you figure you want to see the gold alligator? Well, you're sure going to see him whether you want to or not. Get ready! Here he comes!"

He pulled the door open much as the attendant in the bull-fighting arena might open the gate for a bull.

The hair along King's spine seemed to vibrate. He almost stood up. He could see something very dimly. It reminded him, there in the darkness, of a gigantic English bulldog with wide-spread legs and an ugly looking body.

Still, this was different. It was moving forward now. There was a terrific hissing sound. And in the dim light it gleamed a burnished gold!

A giant golden alligator.

An alligator that, when it stood as straight as possible on its four legs, would measure three and a half or four feet in height at the top of the armored back. The beady eyes, set far back over the top of the snout, seemed to glow like hot coals of fire.

The claws were making a scratching sound on the heavy, timbered floor. King struggled to get free. But he couldn't move.

The alligator must be twenty-five feet in length and enormous in girth. Large enough, King decided, to swallow two or three men whole without causing him stomach trouble.

The tail was lashing slowly back and forth like the tail of a nervous cat.

Once, twice, he shut his eyes and shook his head. Then he opened them again to make sure it wasn't a dream.

But still it came on, inexorably.

It reached a point perhaps five feet from King's legs and stopped there. Crouched as if to spring. The legs which had held the belly off the floor with good clearance now relaxed and the monster settled on its stomach.

There came a hiss like the steam from a locomotive. King could feel the air spraying him from the nostrils of that wicket snout.

The animal lifted its belly from the floor and came on a step or two nearer. King drew back his legs. He felt cold chills running up and down his spine.

THE CREATURE stopped less than three feet away from him.

A harsh, rasping voice filled the room.

"Be warned!"

King stiffened.

The voice continued.

"You have seen two men killed by the Order of the Golden

Alligator. I did not kill them. You will be killed, too, if you do not do what you are told."

"What do you want?" King demanded.

"The Golden Alligator wishes your cooperation in finding the hundred million dollars in gold that is buried off the Florida coast. You, as leader of the Secret 6, will have the confidence of the only man living who knows where the gold is hidden. If you cooperate with us we will divide the treasure fifty-fifty."

"And if I don't?" King hurled back.

"If you refuse," said the voice, "then look into the jaws of the golden alligator and judge for yourself."

The great mouth opened. Those jaws were parted at least three feet wide. There were rows and rows of teeth. Teeth gold like the rest of the monster. Then suddenly the jaws snapped together again with a sharp crack that echoed throughout the building.

"With one movement of the jaws you will be crushed to death," said the voice. "Perhaps you would like to see a demonstration. You shall see the power of those jaws. You think, perhaps, this is a trick. There before you is a board lying on the floor. It looks like tough wood. We'll see."

The eyes of the alligator shifted as the weird human voice out of nowhere filled the room. Shifted toward a loose board just to the left of King's feet.

The monster was rising on its legs, moving towards the board. It made a sudden lunge and picked it up with its front teeth. Then it raised its snout high in the air, threw it up, and let the board slip between its jaws.

The voice came again. "Now, watch," it said.

114

*Crack!*

The jaws snapped together. The board splintered instantly. Broke in three parts. Each end dropped from either side of the jaws and a smaller piece stayed in the mouth.

The animal gulped. The piece of board in the mouth had vanished inside the monster alligator!

The negro's laugh came to him again. The alligator swung its snout toward King. The tail continued to lash slowly.

"Do you believe me now?" rasped the voice.

King found his throat parched and dry. He gulped to speak. But still he stood his ground.

"What is your answer?" snapped the voice impatiently. "Will you help us get the hundred million?"

"No," said King.

"That's your final answer?"

"Yes," he replied.

All the time he was fumbling with the ropes behind him to get free. That great hissing sound came from the 'gator's nostrils again. It advanced. The jaws opened wide enough to swallow him in one gulp!

# CHAPTER 9
## SWALLOWED ALIVE

THE KNOTS were slipping a little, but the ropes still cut deeply into his wrists. King tugged and pulled with all his might. They slipped a little more. Or was that because they were digging deeper into the flesh?

The alligator took one short step and its jaws opened wider. King kicked at it. Kicked again. One foot landed with a crash on the front of the upper jaw of the 'gator; the impact stung him but seemed to have no effect on the beast.

He was sure now that the ropes were slipping a little around his wrists. At the same instant he heard the giant negro at the other end of the great barren space laugh hideously. Then the voice came to him once more.

"I will give you one more chance to agree to help us. If you do not accept now, the golden alligator will advance. I will not hold him back longer. What is your answer?" demanded the voice. "Will you help us? Think well—this is your last chance."

The skin on King's wrists was torn raw from his straining on the ropes but one hand was almost free. If he could get that loose then the other should come easy.

But where was the man whose voice was filling the room?

King must not let him know that he was getting free. The knowledge that his one hand was almost out gave him courage—turned despair into desperate hope. But it would take him a few seconds longer. Play for time. That was his only chance.

He answered the voice now—answered in a dry, choking voice that was almost a sob. He must act the part.

"I've got to have time to think this out," he said.

"Five seconds," echoed the voice. "That is all."

"I've got to have longer than that!" King yelled. "There are too many things to consider."

"Five seconds," the voice insisted.

King didn't answer that last. He was too busy struggling. His sense of time told him, almost to the dot, of the passing of each one of those five precious seconds. Three—four passed.

He managed to get one hand free! The rope spread about his other wrist. The voice broke the silence.

"Your time is up! Let me hear your answer instantly. I cannot hold the golden alligator back any longer."

At the same time the 'gator before him hissed. King could feel the hot breath on his face.

His other hand was almost free.

The alligator raised itself up. The tail was lashing faster.

"Your answer!" rasped the voice.

In that instant the alligator lunged to seize his legs! King wrenched with all his might. His other hand came free!

He was up on his feet in a split second. The gigantic gold front teeth of the monster scratched his legs as he jumped away.

Everything seemed to be confusion. The voice raised to an angry pitch now.

"Stop him! Stop him!" it called. "He's loose."

The golden alligator was snapping at his heels as King ran for the farthest corner. In the dim light he was searching everywhere for the door through which they must have entered. But he couldn't find it. There seemed to be none except the one through which the alligator had come.

A bellow of rage came from the throat of the negro. He tore after King across the dimly-lighted room.

"Stop! Or I'll kill you!" he bellowed.

King looked back in time to see the black man taking something from his pocket. He was whirling it around his head. It was another flying garrote!

The negro clutched one of the little golden alligators in his great fist. He whirled the wire about his head and the gold weight at the other end kept the wire taut.

As yet King was fifteen or twenty feet from the corner. The 'gator and the black man were close behind.

Then that swishing sound that came like a throbbing whisper. It was coming straight for King on a dead level with his throat. He couldn't see the wire. But he saw the glint of the little golden alligators at either end of it.

Round and round that death machine whirled. Came at him with tremendous speed and deadly aim.

There were only two things that he could do. He might duck low; that would slow his forward speed and give the 'gator a chance to catch up with him.

On the other hand he might stand still and throw his arms up over his head to keep the wire from striking his neck and throat. There was not time for him to deliberate.

He threw his arms up over his head, and dropped his chin to avoid the wire from crossing his throat.

*Wam!*

The wire struck with terrific force. Struck his up-raised arms just above the pits. There came a singing sound as though some-one had picked a tightly drawn E string on a mandolin.

Then the whispering of death rose to a higher note. But still very soft. That was the sound made by the weights flying round and round him at the end of the taut wire. In spite of the clothing that he wore he felt the wire cutting through his flesh as it tightened. He dropped his hands as fast as he could, found the two golden alligators at the ends of the wire and flung them around his body in the opposite direction from which they had wound.

The tension of the wire lessened. It fell down around his legs and he tried to run on. But the wire caught and tripped him. He plunged headlong on the rough board floor.

King rolled as he fell to gain a little headway. He was kicking like mad to free his legs from the entanglement of the wire.

Somehow, he got free. The front teeth of the alligator's jaw snapped against the side of one shoe as he leaped up and tore part of the leather from it.

Then something else happened to add more horror to the situation.

Up to then the place had been illuminated dimly by a small light up behind the pillar to which King had been tied. With an abruptness that was as nerve-wracking as the burst of a bomb, that one light went out!

The entire place was plunged into pitch darkness except for two glowing spots that were gaining upon King—the two gleaming eyes of the golden alligator set wide apart on the top of the flat head.

He heard the alligator hiss again as he lunged once more. He heard the claws scratch the hard surface of the floor. Both the alligator and the negro were almost upon him.

King was still going. But now in the darkness he could see nothing but those two eyes of the monster.

King kicked out as the golden jaws opened wide.

*Wam!*

He slammed into the side of the building with terrific force. By some miracle his head escaped striking the heavy beams.

He whirled and darted to the left as the jaws of the alligator snapped at the place where he had been but a second before.

His senses told him that he was fleeing into a trap. He thrust his hands out before him. And just in time.

*Crack!*

His body slammed against another side of the building. He was in a corner.

The negro couldn't seem to see any better than King could. He heard the big black crash against the side of the building, close to him.

But the alligator could tell where it was, apparently. It followed relentlessly. Hissing. Lashing the floor with its tail. Gnashing its teeth.

Then there came another sound—that of splintering, crashing wood. And the beam of a flashlight probed the darkness, blinding King. Other flashlights pricked the inky blackness and one of them caught the huge negro. Then an angry yell echoed in the high timbers—a familiar voice!

There was a flash. A long pencil-like dart slithered out three or four feet in front of the flashlights.

*Blam!*

A gun had gone off.

*Blam!*

Another barked, and another tongue of flame shot out.

King had just crouched in the corner. At the moment that all this had happened he was figuring the possibility of leaping over the alligator and breaking out of his trap.

But suddenly the alligator swerved toward the negro. A perfect bedlam of sounds echoed through the room.

*Blam!*

Another shot sounded as the light riveted on the gold back of the monster.

*Ping!*

The bullet that had apparently struck the great beast somewhere along its back ricocheted and plunked into the heavy, timbered side of the building. The jaws of the 'gator snapped. The hissing sound came.

King leaped out of the corner.

"This way, master!" shouted the voice as King lunged out of the corner.

It was the voice of Luga!

*Blam! Blam!*

GUNS SPOKE again. King heard a deep-throated cry of pain. He turned around as he ran. In the light of the electric torches, he saw that the big black murderer had spun round and clutched his shoulder.

He was down on one knee, struggling to get up and all this time the voice that had come from nowhere was shouting orders.

Now for the first time King heard that rasping voice distinctly. "Get him! Eat him!" it bellowed.

He couldn't tell whether the voice meant that the alligator was supposed to get him or not. If so, there was a misunderstanding somewhere, for the 'gator lunged at the falling negro murderer. He saw the jaws open wide—saw them grasp the negro by the legs. The negro's arms went up over his head. A scream of terror left his lips.

Then out before the other flashlights Luga came tearing. He clutched at the other black who was being gulped down by the alligator—clutched him by both arms and pulled with all his might.

The enormous throat gulped. The black garrote-thrower shot down the huge throat! And Luga was forced to let go to save himself from following into those deadly jaws.

King grasped Luga.

"Get out of here," King said. "That thing will eat us all alive if we aren't—"

The noise of guns cut him off. Tongues of flames pierced the darkness. Flames that hurled straight for the jaws of the gold alligator.

*Ping! Ping! Ping!*

Bullets made a whistling sound as they ricocheted off the monster's back. In spite of the fact that the alligator had swallowed a huge man alive, it was traveling rapidly toward the door at the other end of the warehouse through which it had entered.

The voices of the other members of the Secret 6 came to King. They were all about him. He heard the Doctor yell, "Stop that thing!" The Bishop said something he couldn't catch. It sounded like a prayer. Then he saw the gun in the Bishop's hand spit flame three times.

Luga raced ahead to try to change the course of the great beast. The tail of the monster caught Luga's legs from the side as he ran. Sent him sprawling. Nothing would stop the flight of the golden alligator.

It had almost reached the low wide door.

Now it was half way through the opening.

The Doctor was beside King. Characteristic of a man of his profession, he asked breathlessly, "Are you hurt, King?"

"No," King answered. Then they were bending double, diving through that low door behind the fleeing alligator. The light of the Doctor was showing them the way.

As King and the Doctor rushed through together King could feel the cooler, livelier air of the night on his face. He heard the sound of water close by and the darkness increased to such an extent all they could see was the gleam of the golden alligator as it vanished down the dock. Suddenly the Doctor grasped King by the arm.

"Stop!" he shouted. "That's open water there."

He was pointing toward the darker space that his light did not penetrate. They stopped together.

*Blam! Blam!*

The Doctor let go two last shots at the fleeing alligator. Then King shouted.

"Look! The beast is going down that ramp into the water!"

He and the Doctor were both standing stock still now—staring in awe and horror.

"He's got that big black fella inside of him!" King exclaimed.

The others of the Secret 6 caught up and stood about.

"Yeah," said the Key sarcastically. "I should think you'd be crying your eyes out about that. After all that big mug did to you."

King didn't answer for a moment. He was staring with bulging eyes. He saw the 'gator slip into the water. Saw it submerge and the tail vanish. Then, except for the rolling of the low waves in the light of the electric torches, all seemed calm and peaceful. For a moment no one spoke. Then King found words.

"I was trying to save that black. Not for himself," he said. "That fella deserves to die if anyone does. I was hoping, though, that we could kill that alligator and cut the black fella out of his stomach. It might have been possible that he wasn't dead. If we could have got him alive we might have wrung a confession out of him. That was all I was after."

"Fat chance," said the Key. "Don't forget, King, when that 'gator took his last gulp that black boy was as dead as they make them."

King walked on a little farther.

"Come on, Doctor," he said. "Let's cast that light of yours around here and see if we can find out where that monster comes up."

"You'll have a time doing that," said the Doctor. "That thing can stay down a long time if it wants to. But I never heard of alligators in the East River."

"Is that where we are?" King asked.

"Sure," he said. "Didn't you know? We're down on the south Brooklyn side. This place is an old dock and warehouse that hasn't been used for a long time. You don't mean to say that they knocked you unconscious before they brought you here?"

"I don't know whether it was intentional or not," King replied. "I'm more inclined to think it was an accident. I think when that big colored man ran out of the police station I hit my head on the edge of the car when he threw me into the back seat."

"That's right," the Key said.

"How do you know?" he demanded.

The Key opened his mouth to answer. Then suddenly he stopped short.

"*Shhhh,*" he said. "Pipe down and listen."

EVERY MEMBER of the Secret 6 tensed there at the edge of the water. They could hear sounds of heavy footsteps plainly in the warehouse that they had just left. Then very dimly they heard voices.

"Are you sure this is the place, inspector?" they heard someone say.

A muffled, growling answer came. King thought there was something familiar about that voice. Then he decided he must be wrong. Perhaps it was some police officer's voice he had heard in the past.

"There ain't nothing here?" they heard someone else say.

The heavy footsteps were coming nearer to the opening through which the Secret 6 had followed the alligator.

"Holy gee!" the Key whispered. "It's the cops. Douse those lights!"

All the lights went out as the Key spoke and every eye was on that door. They saw lights inside swing around near it.

"If they come out here," the Key whispered, "we're sunk!"

"Unless," King shot back, "we can swim."

"You mean swim in that water with the alligator taking a bath at the same time?" the Key demanded in a very low voice.

"Maybe," said the Doctor, "you'd rather go back and offer to show the police over the Brooklyn dock area."

The voices were coming closer.

"Hey," one said, "maybe this is the right place. Look at this post. Somebody's been tied up. Here's the rope still hanging on it."

Silence for a moment.

King was searching frantically for some place on the dock where they might hide. Now, with their flashes out he could hardly see.

Out in the East River the lights of ships gleamed, and across it towered the great buildings of Manhattan with lights glowing in thousands of windows. Another voice boomed from inside the warehouse.

"Look over here. This is the place all right. Here's blood on the floor."

Lights gleamed through the open door now.

He reached the end of the
wharf and peered around one
of the pilings cautiously.

"There's nothing more in here. They've gone somewhere," someone observed.

"Yeah," said another. "Out that door. Let's see what's outside. Have your guns ready. This Secret 6 is a desperate crowd."

King shrugged in the darkness.

"Well, Key," he whispered. "I guess that's your cue. Personally, I'm going to take to the water. You can do what you want to."

Already Shakespeare, the Doctor and the Bishop were slipping over the edge of the dock into the water as noiselessly as possible.

"Hurry!" hissed King. "Here they come!"

As King spoke he slipped over the edge of the dock. Luga was beside him. He heard the Key whisper, "I think I'll take the water, too. Gee! But I'll bet it's going to be cold."

All six were now in the water. The sound of heavy feet on the dock came to them as the police stepped outside the low door.

King whispered an order.

"Duck under the dock and hold onto the piling."

They obeyed and hung far back into the shadows. Looking up through the cracks of the heavy boards that formed the dock, King could see rays of the light the police carried.

The water was cold. Almost like ice. He clinched his teeth tight to keep them from chattering. His loyal men of the Secret 6, each clinging to a piling that supported the dock were all about him.

The police were *directly* above them now. King couldn't tell the exact number, but it seemed like a regular riot squad.

"They must have got away in a boat," one of them said.

"That'd be just our luck."

"I'll bet if we'd got here ten minutes earlier we'd seen some fun."

"That blood in there on the floor wasn't spilled over five minutes ago. They couldn't be very far away," another said.

"Say, I got an idea," said one of the cops. "You wait here to see if anything happens and I'll go out to the nearest 'phone and have the office get in touch with the patrol boat out in the river. We'll round them up that way. We'll stop every suspicious looking craft we find."

"Okay. Make it snappy."

THEY WAITED while the Secret 6 under their feet fairly froze as they hung onto the piling. Then very softly King heard the throbbing of a powerful engine nearby. An engine with an underwater exhaust. The Doctor was nearest him. King hung onto his piling with one hand and touched the Doctor's shoulder with the other.

"Hear that?" King asked in an almost inaudible whisper.

"Yes," the Doctor hissed hack. "Where do you figure it is?"

"Out at the end of the wharf," King said. "Wait here. I'm going to swim out and see if I can get sight of it. I'd gamble that boat holds the entire secret of what we want to know."

"Good luck!" the Doctor whispered.

King struck out in a silent but powerful breast stroke. He could see fairly well now from the reflection of light that shone down through the cracks of the dock.

A moment later he heard a scuffling of feet overhead. The cops were following along just above him.

"What's that?" one demanded.

King slowed his movements and merely floated. Could it be possible that they could hear him swimming?

"That engine out there somewhere. It's not very far away."

"It sounds like it's down at the end of the dock here."

"Hey, Jerry," said another in a hoarse whisper. "Slip back and 'phone the office to wireless the patrol boats to be on the lookout for a craft just leaving the end of this pier."

"And don't spare the horses," said another. "I think we're going to catch them."

King swam on. It was hard work, this silent swimming with his clothes bound tightly around his jaw.

The coolness of the water chilled his muscles. Almost froze him to the bone. He resented the slapping sound that the water was making against the piling at the side of the wharf. The cops were walking over the top of his head.

He heard them passing him now. King couldn't hope to keep up with their fast walking without making more noise. Then the cops were running. He heard them ahead. They had reached the end of the dock. One of them shouted.

"There she is! Running without lights. She just left the end of the pier!

"Hey, you out there in that boat without any lights, stop or we'll fire!"

The only response was the roar of powerful engines in the craft.

*Blam! Blam! Blam!* Cracked the guns of the police.

King was swimming for all he was worth now. No need to muffle his sound any longer. The shouting and confusion and throbbing of those engines were making it impossible for the men above him to hear his movements.

He reached the end of the wharf and peered cautiously around one of the pilings. He could just see the boat pulling out into the river in a V of spray. He could see enough of it to know that it was a big craft—a high-powered, fast-moving express cruiser.

But seeing it from the stern he couldn't tell much about the type or the length. He half turned to go back. The boat was out of sight. There was no need of staying there any longer.

Then, as he reached out in a stroke, his hand touched something that was floating on the water. At first he discarded it.

There was always junk of every kind floating around in the East River.

He touched it again and his hand came in contact with a handle. He held fast now. Felt over it. His heart leaped—he had touched a suitcase floating in the water, half-submerged.

He clung to the handle and started back for the place where he had left the others. The police were running back the way they had come. Then suddenly a searchlight turned on the whole wharf from out on the river.

"Here we are," he heard one of the cops yell.

King ducked behind a piling and tried to stay there out of the light. He hoped that the others would do the same.

The boat with the light was thundering toward the dock. King held his position behind that piling. Peering to one side of it, he saw the hulk of a police patrol boat. The searchlight was turned on the police officer.

"You got the message?" one of them called.

"Yeah," sang back one of the men on the boat. "Just came over the wireless this minute."

There was the clatter of feet as the men hopped aboard. The great engine in the police boat roared. Backed out of the slip.

"It went down that way," King heard someone say.

ALL THE police officers were on board now except the two who had been sent to telephone. The boat started out into the river at full throttle. But already the throbbing sound of the other boat—that one that King took for a fast express cruiser—was dying away in the distance. It was headed for the harbor entrance and the open sea.

King clutched the suitcase and swam on. He reached the point where he had left the others of the Secret 6.

"Let's get out of here," the Key hissed. "The cops are all gone now."

"Okay," said King. "But we've got to take it easy. Two of them ought to be back any minute."

He was just about to raise up and look over the edge of the dock when he heard the sound of running footsteps. He ducked low and tensed, still holding the suitcase. Someone was coming out on the dock.

*"Huummm,"* he heard a man say, "that was fast work. The patrol boat must have picked them up already. Well, that lets me out. Guess I'll go back to headquarters."

The man strode away.

A moment later they heard voices again. This time, inside the wharf. King listened. This first one to come back had probably been the first to leave and apparently he was meeting the other one returning. He strained his ears to catch what was said.

"They've gone on the patrol boat," he heard the one say.

"Might as well go back to headquarters. There's nothing going on here."

"Okay," said the other. "Glad to get out of this hole. These docks give me the willies, anyway."

King waited a full minute after he heard their footsteps die away. Then he called softly to the others.

"Everybody here?"

"I believe so," said the Bishop. "I'm ha-half frozen. I sug-sug-gest we get out of this water."

"Me, too," ventured the Key.

KING TOSSED the soggy suitcase up on top of the dock and pulled himself over. Luga and the Doctor came up beside him. Those three on top came to the others and helped them up over the edge.

When they were all standing there in the darkness, dripping with clammy cold water of the East River, King counted the figures.

"One, two, three, four, five," he said. "And I make six. Everybody here, Shakespeare?"

"Yes, my lord," said Shakespeare's voice.

"Key?"

"Check," said the Key.

"Doctor?"

"Right."

"Bishop?"

"Here."

"Luga?"

"Yes, master."

"Okay. Let's go. Have we got a car anywhere around here?"

"Yes," said the Key. "And I'm speaking first for the blanket in back seat, too. Don't forget that."

"I think," said the Bishop, "we can all use that blanket!"

King went first down the dock, carrying the suitcase into the warehouse. The police might have left a guard, but he doubted it from the conversation he had overheard.

"Shine your flashlight around for once, just for fun."

The Doctor obliged.

"It's a good thing," he said, "we use water-proof flashlights."

"I saw to that in the beginning," said the Bishop.

"How did you get in here?" asked King.

Luga pointed over, to a far corner opposite to the corner where King had been trapped when they came in.

"Door over there," he said. "We come in that way."

"Okay," said King. "We'll follow. But make it snappy. I'm freezing in these wet clothes."

The faithful black went at a dog-trot. Luga found the door. He flung it open and they passed through, out into the night again.

The great black led them up a dinky, narrow side-street. One car was parked by the curb. Places of business were there, but they were all shrouded in darkness.

The six men climbed into the car. King took the wheel. With teeth chattering a chorus they started off, swung up the street through the more populated area, and out into the suburbs. At length they turned on the north shore main highway and headed for the jungle camp.

As they drove, the Doctor asked King a question.

"What was that thing I saw you carrying from the dock?"

"It's a small suitcase. It may not mean anything, but I picked it up. It was floating, half-submerged, out at the end of the dock."

"Did you get a good look at the boat that left?" the Bishop chattered.

"No," said King. "I made a guess that it's a high-powered express cruiser. But it may be fifty feet long or it may be a hundred and fifty feet long. It's plenty fast, that's all I do know." The Secret 6 finished their journey in silence to the hidden cabin.

When they reached the cabin, Luga built a roaring fire in the fireplace. They took off their soaked clothing and hung them up to dry. King put on his pajamas. The Bishop's eyes twinkled.

"I'm very glad to see that move, King," he said. "We've lost a lot of sleep tonight so far, and I, for one, think we'd be better off if we'd all take a wink or so before we go into this matter."

"That's what I'm going to do," King said with determination. "I stumbled on this thing originally because I dozed off to sleep when I was driving last night. 'Course, that dip in the East River helped to wake me up a little bit."

"We'll all be lucky," growled the Doctor, "if we don't catch our death of cold from that dip. And, King, if you hadn't decided to turn in for a few winks I was going to make you. As a doctor, I've got to look after the physical welfare of you men, whether you like it or not."

King yawned.

"You won't have to, Doctor, in my case, as far as sleep is concerned. Because I'm turning in right now."

"Say, wait a minute—you can't drop off just like that."

"Yes," said the Bishop. "I was wondering about that, too. Don't you think we ought to have a look at the suitcase that you found? That might mean something."

"That's one thing I was going to do before I turned in," King answered.

Already he was fumbling with the latch of the small, water-soaked suitcase. He tried three times to open the lock, gave it up and turned to Luga.

"The thing is locked," he said. "Hand me that big screwdriver over there, will you, Luga?"

"Yes, master."

King took the big screwdriver and wrenched the lock open. It was a cheap affair and it took little prying to tear the whole front open. King threw back the lid and examined the interior. The others were standing about, watching him as he worked.

At first it appeared that there were only clothes in it. King picked out a shirt that was roughly folded on top and held it before him.

"Phew! This shirt belongs to a big man."

"Did belong to him," the Key corrected.

It was far too big for King. He walked over to Luga and held it up before him. It was a fairly easy fit for the giant black Zulu chief.

"Try it on," King suggested. "It's yours, Luga, if you want it. I'll bet there aren't many men who could fill that shirt."

Luga had stripped his clothes off and now had the pants of pajamas on below his waist. He was naked above. He unbuttoned the great shirt and slipped it on. Everyone watched.

"Shoulders a little big. Neck about right. Who do you think owned this shirt, master? Must be big man."

King smiled.

"Who do you think, Luga?" he asked.

"Maybe, another black man."

"That's my guess, too."

"Jolly!" exclaimed the Bishop. "It would seem then that we ought to find something in this suitcase that would give us a lead."

"That's what I'm hoping," said King, continuing to go through the clothes as he dumped them out on the table. There were neckties, and underwear and shirts and more shirts—all of that huge size.

"I'll bet," King ventured, "this fellow had to have his things made to order. I was wondering about you, Luga. You're getting out of clothes. I think you can wear these very well. And it'll save us having some made for you."

"Yes, master," said Luga. "Luga like very much."

"Don't tell me," demanded the Doctor, "that you can't find any evidence in that suitcase?"

"Not yet," King replied. "Wait—I'm almost down to the bottom now. Here's something. What's this?"

He took out a folded paper. It was rather large and bulky, folded in a compact size.

*"Hummm,"* he said, half to himself. "A road map. A road map of Florida. Well, this is certainly interesting."

Together they pored over it in the light.

"Maybe this will help us get straightened out on the situation down there ourselves," King said. "Let's see now. Everglades City should be somewhere along the southwest coast. Down among these Ten Thousand—"

"Jolly!" exclaimed the Bishop. "There's a cross down there. Is that where Everglades City is?"

King took a closer look.

"That's right. That's Everglades City marked with a cross. I don't suppose any of you have ever been down there?"

He glanced about. No one had.

"It is evident," he continued, "that the person who had this suitcase was thinking of going there—thinking very seriously of it."

"That seems obvious," said Shakespeare. "And you think that the huge colored man whom the alligator swallowed *is* the one who owned the suitcase?"

"He's the only one I can think of. It looks to me as though he had his suitcase down there ready to leave. Then the alligator suddenly pulled a dirty trick on him and gobbled him up. At any rate, it's nice to know that the flying garrote murderer is done for."

"Right," said the Doctor. "But where do we go from here? We've evidence that this big colored fellow—the murderer, I mean—was heading for Florida. Naturally, that's the land of the alligator in the United States. But the man we're after is the brains of the whole organization."

"Suppose King you tell us what's been going on since we saw you last."

"I think it would be better," King said, "if the Key told what he knew. Then I can tie my story up with his."

The Key grinned and cleared his throat. Lighted a fresh cigarette.

"Sure," he said. "I'll tell you what little I know. It won't help you much."

King smiled.

"But not now, Key," he said. "Let's wait until tomorrow morning. I'll be able to think more clearly when I get some rest."

"But," ventured the Doctor, "perhaps you or the Key will have some information that'll fit together and demand instant action."

"I don't think so," said King. "Sometime tomorrow we all start for Florida. I'll explain why in the morning. Goodnight, gentlemen."

## CHAPTER 10
## THE COFFIN FLIGHT

NEXT TO Luga, King was first to rise next morning. It was barely daylight. The sun was just rimming the horizon through the trees, coming up like a great gold disc, as though it were rising directly out of the Sound.

The loyal black man was preparing breakfast silently. He glanced over at King.

"Good morning, master," he said.

"Good morning, Luga," came the answer. "All set for a long hop this morning?"

"Yes, master," said Luga. "Luga like to ride in airplane."

The sleepy voice of the Doctor came now.

"Say," he said with an anxious note, "isn't there some way I can get to Florida without flying?"

"Plenty of ways," said King. "But there aren't any ways of getting down there as fast as we've got to travel unless you fly."

The Doctor groaned.

"And I swore I'd never fly in an airplane!"

King laughed.

"What is there about an airplane that makes you so skittish?" he demanded.

The Doctor shook his head. "I don't know," he said. "I'll travel any other way, but not by air. If anything happens up there you seem so helpless. Maybe I could make it soon enough in a train."

King shrugged.

"It's O.K. with me. We can meet you at Everglades City, if you like."

The Doctor smiled with relief.

Getting up, he examined the map that King had left on the table, and discovered that Everglades City was only about sixty or seventy miles from Miami.

"I can hire a car in Miami and be there in an hour or two after

I get off the train," he said emphatically. "That is, shortly after noon tomorrow."

He brought out a Gladstone bag and packed it hurriedly. He sat down to breakfast before the others were ready and in less than a half hour was ready to leave. He paused at the door, bag in hand.

"Where shall we meet?" he asked.

"Better ask for John Hernando," King said. "We'll probably be tying up with him for the time being."

The Doctor nodded.

"Very well. And I'll take the roadster in case you want to use the sedan. Goodbye and good luck! See you tomorrow."

The others sat down to a more leisurely breakfast than their colleague had eaten. As he cut into a juicy sausage, King turned to the Key.

"There are some things I want to ask you. I sent you to trail this fellow, John L. Ogden. What did you learn?"

The Key's thin face fell.

"Well, gee, King, I meant to."

King glared at him.

"Meant to?" he snapped. "You didn't follow him?"

"Well, not exactly," said the Key. "Or, that is, I did follow him for a ways."

"What happened?"

"Well, that was kind of funny. Almost all the rest of the guys had cars. The financier had a—"

"What was so funny about what Ogden did?" King interrupted.

"Well, I kind of got surprised there," the Key said. "I figured he was a gangster, but I couldn't place him. Naturally I expected he'd have a couple of guards waiting for him at the door and they'd all climb in a bullet-proof limousine or something. Instead of that, he goes mogging up the street like he didn't have a thing to do in the world and all the time to do it in.

"I followed him for about a half a block and then I heard the police siren. And darned if the cops' car didn't stop right out in front of the Altoona Hotel.

"So I ran back, thinking maybe there was something up. But, gee, I didn't mean to lose sight of Ogden. The only thing I was thinking of when I heard the cops coming was maybe you was in trouble. I got up on your floor and found they were in your room."

KING'S EYES narrowed.

"Was that you down at the end of the hall?" he demanded. "I saw a shadow there move a little bit."

The Key nodded sheepishly.

"Yep. That was me. I tried to get up to your room to warn you. But I couldn't get ahead of the cops. So I figured there wasn't any use of getting caught with you. I just stood in a doorway and then I trailed you to see what station they took you to. Then I got hold the Dummy and told him to send a message by short wave and tell the gang to get into the station as soon as they could. And I'd wait.

"That took me an awful long time. Because I had to hunt for the Dummy and then the gang had to get collected and drive in. But they got to the station after that big guy from Harlem had snatched you and killed a lot of cops.

"I trailed him and the car to see where they took you. I left the Dummy there at the station and told him I'd call and let them know where we were after they'd stopped with you. That's how we all got together down at the Brooklyn wharves."

"And you didn't trail Ogden any farther than a half a block?"

"Gee, chief," said the Key, "I'm—I'm awfully sorry. But honest, I thought I was doing the right thing by trying to keep track of you."

King smiled and planted a playful punch against the shoulder of the dejected Key.

"The way it worked out," he said, "I guess you did just the right thing, Key. Because if you hadn't trailed me to the East River wharf the chances are I'd be reposing very quietly in the stomach of that golden alligator. I doubt very much if I'd ever have gotten out without your help."

"Gee! That's swell," said the Key. "Then you don't hold it against me?"

"Sure," said King. "I hold it against you just like anybody would have it in for somebody who had saved his life. Don't be ridiculous."

"And what happened," said the Bishop, "to you?"

"Plenty," said King. "After the Key and I left here we went to the Altoona Hotel.

"I found the list of names, together with the men's addresses and telephone numbers. So I 'phoned each man, told him I was Hernando and that I wanted to see him as soon as possible."

"I assume," said Shakespeare, "you suspect that one of those six men is the guilty party behind all this trouble."

King was non-committal, but it was significant that he described each one of them to the members of the Secret 6 who were there.

When he had finished, the Bishop said, "One would assume from your description that you suspect this man named Ogden, who calls himself a merchant."

"There's something very funny about him," King admitted. "There's no doubt about that. On the other hand, there's something else that sticks in my crop."

The Key turned to him quickly.

"You mean, you got reason to suspect one of the others?"

King shrugged.

"I don't know. Here's one thing that hasn't been answered yet. You know what the cops arrested me for when they came up in the room?"

The Key shook his head.

"They arrested me for murder."

"Murder!" gasped the Bishop.

"Yes. For the murder of Close."

"That's strange," said Shakespeare. "How could any of them know that you were with Close when he was murdered?"

"I told all six of them that I was with Close when he was murdered," King said. "As far as I know, no one else knew."

The Bishop's eyes twinkled. "Except," he ventured, "the murderer."

King nodded. "You've hit it there," he said. "That's what I want to know. The murderer was the one who called the police from the hotel. By having me arrested for the murder that would let him out without a chance of suspicion."

The Key stared at him.

"Holy gee! You mean you think one of those guys called the police and sicked them on you the minute he got out of your room?"

"That's it.

"Can you figure out which one that might have been, Key? Just think back now and see if you can remember any of the six going to a telephone booth in the hotel."

The Key assumed a posture of deep thinking. Then he began to do it out loud.

"Let's see, now," he said. "I saw the six of them come down in the same elevator. Ogden stepped out of the elevator and looked around the lobby. He was taking plenty of time. I watched him while he went over to the cigar stand and bought a pocket full of cigars."

"How long did that take?" King asked.

"Oh, I don't know," said the Key. "Maybe five or six minutes."

"Then what happened?" King asked.

"WELL," THE Key went on, "Ogden started out. The rest of them seemed to stop for this and that here and there. I don't know but that they stopped to talk in the lobby for a few minutes.

"I saw Stanton start down the street hoofing it when we got outside. That big financier and that cocky little banker, whatever his name was, were waiting for their chauffeur-driven busses to pull up.

"Then the doctor. His coupé pulled up with its chauffeur and he got in and drove away."

"That leaves Freeman, the headmaster of the school. You say you don't remember much about him?" King asked.

"I don't remember seeing him talking in the group that stopped in the lobby. Gee! I wish you'd told me to watch the others closer."

"I figured you'd only be able to handle one at a time."

He pushed back his plate, lighted a cigar, and looked thoughtfully into the smoke.

"Well," he said, "I wonder if Ogden was the only man out of the whole six honest men who could have put in that telephone call?"

"If one of them did call," the Bishop corrected.

"I can't see," said King, "how it can be figured any other way. There isn't a single doubt in my mind but what some of those men who were in that room with us up there are behind this Order of the Golden Alligator."

"Do you think," asked Shakespeare, "that he had any idea that you were connected with the Secret 6?"

King shook his head.

"Not in the slightest," he said.

"Why?" asked the Bishop.

"Because," said King. "Even after the police put me behind the bars they weren't sure that I was connected with the Secret 6."

"But someone must have recognized your face," ventured Shakespeare.

King smiled.

"They sure did," he said. "Several of them. Then they tried to check that with my fingerprints and that's what knocked them all haywire. My fingerprints didn't rack up with my face.

"I gave them a story about having been taken before for King of the Secret 6 because of our facial resemblance. And I honestly believe that they partially believed me. But they weren't taking any chances and from what I understood they had this telephone call telling them I had murdered Close.

"So they had enough on me to hang me if they could find the witnesses to it even without connecting me with King of the Secret 6 in the least."

The others pushed back from the table. King sat smoking silently. He heard the Bishop chuckle.

"I was just thinking," said the Bishop, "isn't it strange sometimes how we run across a man we are absolutely positive has done a certain thing—and then an investigation proves he is the only one who possibly couldn't have done it?"

"Like Ogden?" King asked.

"Yes," said the Bishop.

"I was thinking of that," said King, "when you spoke. And here's another very strange thing that I'd like to understand better. There seems to be a little rivalry somewhere in this business."

"What do you mean?" asked the Key.

"Just this," said King, "Who told the police to come to the wharf last night? Now the Order of the Golden Alligator was running the whole show—there's not the slightest doubt about it. And certainly they didn't call the police and tell them to come down and arrest themselves. Someone else must have tipped them off."

He shrugged and held out his hands in a baffled gesture.

"You see what I mean?" he asked. "It sounds as though we aren't the only ones fighting the Golden Alligator. There is another faction—and last night they were forced to help us—but who are they?"

"MAYBE ITS just the cops," the Key ventured.

"I hardly think so," said King. "Although it might be someone working with the police."

"Say, listen," said the Key abruptly. "I've been thinking about this guy Ogden. You say he's the only one who couldn't have 'phoned because I was watching him all the time. Well, listen. He looked like a pretty smooth duck to me. Suppose he suspected that he was being watched. Maybe there was someone at the cigar counter that he knew and he told him to call the police."

King nodded.

"That certainly sounds possible," he said.

"Then," smiled the Bishop, "we have this much to go on—which is less than we had before. Assuming that last statement of yours, Key, is possible. It's highly probable that anyone of the six men who met you and King in John Hernando's room could have called up the police, or at least have been instrumental in warning them."

"I'm afraid that's true," said King. "All of which puts our friend, John L. Ogden, who acts more like J. L. Sullivan, back in the limelight."

King began dressing.

"What do we do next?" the Key asked.

"I think," King said, "we'd better just stay here." Then he laughed. "I don't mean that as bluntly as it sounded. I'm going down to Brooklyn. While I'm gone the rest of you will have time to pack up what clothing you want to take along to Florida. We'll take off when I get back."

"Meaning when?" asked the Key.

"Oh, possibly by noon."

The Bishop's eyes twinkled.

"I'm afraid I'll never grow up," he said. "But after all I can't help being curious about what you're going to do."

"That's very simple," King told him. "I'm going to lower Brooklyn to see if I can learn who has rented the warehouse that the Order of the Golden Alligator used for their show last night.

"Then, there's John Hernando's body. I haven't quite forgotten that. In all due respect to his uncle, I think it's no more than right that we should take the body back to Florida with us."

The Key shook his head.

"I suppose you're right. But you sure do think of the pleasantest ways of taking trips sometimes."

"Jolly!" exclaimed the Bishop. "I didn't know this was to be particularly a pleasure trip from any angle."

"It'll be a pleasant trip," King said, "if we get the birds we're after."

"Yes, indeed," said Shakespeare.

Later in the morning, King was driving through lower Brooklyn in the dock section. With some trouble he located the pier and warehouse where the ghastly happenings of the night before had taken place.

He slowed the car and was about to get out and examine the seemingly deserted wharf in the daylight when a heavy-set figure put in an appearance from a door at the street side.

He stepped on the accelerator.

"Good thing I saw that bird in time," he said. "It looks as if the police have a plain clothes man on the job. That would make a nice little party at this stage of the game."

He moved on down the rough, smelly street. It was indeed a tough section. Ugly-looking men lurked about here and there. But King got the number of the pier.

"Funny," he said. "The thing doesn't look as if it's used for anything."

He drove farther around to the business section. Passed some buildings with offices above. He found printed on one window, "Boggs and Glotz, Real Estate." He got out of the car and climbed the stairs to the office.

A dark little man with curly hair and rather thick glasses bustled up to meet him. He held out his hand.

"Good morning," he said rapidly. "I'm Mr. Glotz of 'Boggs and Glotz.' Is there something we could do for you in the real estate line this morning? Maybe to buy a fine four-family apartment or maybe—"

"I came," King cut in, "to see about leasing a pier."

The eyes of the little man opened wide with hope.

"You want to lease a pier? Are you in the shipping business?"

"I'm planning to go into the shipping business," said King.

The man rubbed his hands together.

"That's fine," he said. "What did you have in mind?"

"Almost all of the piers seem to be taken down along the East River front. But there's one I noticed that didn't seem to have much life about it."

The little man beamed.

"What's the number of the pier, please?"

King gave him the number he had seen in dim paint on the street-end of the pier.

"I'll have it for you in two minutes if it's for lease," said the man, hurrying to his desk and picking up the telephone.

But it was fifteen or twenty minutes before he even found out who owned the pier.

KING WAITED patiently. Everything he wanted to know might be cleared up in the next few minutes. Glotz was calling the owner now. Some steamship company that King had never heard of.

Then Glotz was talking to the president of the company himself.

"I have a client," he said, "who wants to lease your pier. Could you give me the price and terms, please?"

He waited while the answer came back. A frown of hopelessness crossed his face.

"Oh, but that shouldn't matter," he said. "Maybe my client would fix it up himself…. Yes, but listen, maybe we could rent it without saying anything about it…. Oh, I see. You—" He stopped short.

Then slowly he replaced the receiver on the hook.

"He hung up on me," Glotz groaned.

"What did he say," King asked quickly.

"He said the wharf was not for rent. It's been condemned and they haven't used it for two years. They're thinking of fixing it up themselves. It's not for lease."

"Apparently," said King, "it isn't leased to anyone now."

"No," said the other. "I'm sorry. Very sorry, mister. But maybe I could get you a nice pier some other place."

"Sorry," said King. "I was only interested in that one."

The man followed him to the door, still remonstrating.

"Thanks a lot for your trouble, anyway," King told him, smiling as he left.

King drove back to the North highway and watched for the place near young Hernando's body—if it hadn't yet been discovered. He passed through the town where the woman garage-keeper had fixed his car and rented him hers.

If he left the car about a mile or so beyond that town, he should be able to cut across a wooded section and come to the little field where Hernando had been murdered.

He picked a place in the wide gentle ditch, parked the car well off the road and struck off on foot through the woods.

An hour passed in a fruitless search. It was a bit hard to tell the exact spot where Hernando's murder had taken place.

Finally he sighted a slight depression across the field in the weed-strewn grass. Hurried to it. So far as he could tell, he was out of direct sight of any house.

He reached the spot and stared down in astonishment. The

body of young Hernando was there. But it wasn't as King had left it.

The body was stark naked. Hernando's clothing had been stripped from him. Some of it was still there. His coat was gone. King crouched in the low grass.

He wasn't sure now that he wasn't seen. Someone had been there since the murder. One of the members of the Order of the Golden Alligator—or was it this mysterious opposing faction that had come into evidence?

It was certainly obvious that it was someone who was very anxious to learn secrets that John Hernando might carry. But why had they stripped his clothing from his body? King couldn't fathom that.

He put what clothing there was back on the body. At first he didn't dare carry it, for the field where the body lay was out in the open.

So when King had the body dressed he began dragging it toward the woods he had just come through. At the edge of the wood he tossed it over his shoulder and struggled on.

Coming to the side of the road where he had left the car, he laid the body down in the shelter of some bushes. At the time no cars were passing, but it was important to take no chances.

King walked to the car, took out the blanket, and wrapped and securely tied the body. It was stiff as a board.

He lifted it over his arm and walked toward the car when suddenly he heard the rattling of a truck coming down the road—a farmer.

For an instant King hesitated. Then he realized that the

155

farmer had seen him. It would only make matters worse to turn back. He kept on toward the car with the stiff, heavy bundle under his arms.

His nerves were tingling a little, for the truck was slowing down behind his sedan. It was drawing to the side of the road. King tried not to pay any attention to the man. He opened the rear door of the sedan. Put the body in. At least that would give him a chance to get a flying start if he couldn't argue the farmer out of any suspicions that he might have.

KING CLOSED the door. Out of the corner of his eye he saw the farmer climbing out of his truck. He was coming toward him. There was a mean look in his eyes.

"So you're the fella that's been stealing my firewood!" he cried.

King almost blurted out, "Your firewood?" But he didn't quite. Instead he answered with an easy smile.

"Well, I'm certainly sorry. I didn't know it was your firewood or I wouldn't have taken it. I didn't know that anyone cared about the deadwood in this forest."

"It ain't no forest," snapped the farmer. "It's my wood lot. And I'm going to have the law on you unless—"

"Please," King said, "don't get me wrong. I'm no ordinary thief."

"I should say you ain't. You're a lowlived scoundrel. I heard people telling about you coming up here taking wood out. Why, you ain't even man enough to bring it out in broad daylight. You got to cover it up with a blanket."

He was standing close to the closed car, peering in through the window at the blanket.

"Look here," snapped King. "I'm not in the habit of being called a liar and a thief. You name your price for whatever wood you think I've taken out and I'll pay you for it."

The farmer grinned.

"So," he said, "you're getting kind of scared, are you? Well, I don't know as I'd gain anything by putting you in jail so long as you'd pay for it."

"Name your price," said King. "I've got to get back to camp."

"Oh, you one of them fellers about a mile down the road?"

"Yes," said King, not even knowing what the farmer was talking about.

"Well, let's see," said the farmer. "I'm going to make you pay plenty so it'll be a lesson to you. You give me two dollars and we'll call it square."

King found a two dollar bill in his pocket and handed it to the farmer.

"With the greatest of pleasure." And he really meant it. "And may the two dollar bill bring you some good luck."

King turned and climbed into his car. He started the engine. But the farmer didn't leave just then. He was chuckling softly to himself. Chuckling so that King stared at him curiously.

And he couldn't help but turn and ask before he drove away, "Say, what's the joke, anyway?"

The farmer burst out laughing and slapped his leg.

"I was athinking," he said, "some of you city fellers think you're pretty smart when you come up in the country. But I put one over on you this time."

King frowned.

"I don't get it," he said. But he couldn't help but smile at the farmer even though he had a nervous feeling with that stiff corpse in the back seat.

"Ha, ha, ha!" roared the farmer. "That's good. I got the two dollars and you got the wood. And the wood lot don't belong to neither one of us."

"What!" cried King. "You aren't the owner of these woods?"

"Naw," chuckled the other. "I'm just a hired hand working on the Clark place down the road about two miles. Well, so long. Next time you need wood I hope I'll be around to catch you again."

Then he went back to his truck, still shaking with mirth while King drove off with his gruesome load.

When he reached the hiding place of the Secret 6, he turned down the bedrock road with no cars in sight on the main highway. He breathed a little easier then.

He parked the car in the accustomed hiding place and carried the stiff corpse, still done up in the blanket, to the long narrow field. There a six-seated, low-winged plane was staked out under the overhanging trees. He laid the body gently in the aisle between the seats, closed the door and locked it.

Luga, Shakespeare, the Key and the Bishop were waiting for him. A late lunch was still on the table. He sat down and began eating without a great deal of enthusiasm.

"I brought young Hernando's body back," he said. "It's in the plane. I thought I was certainly caught with the goods, too, when I brought it out of the woods and put it in the car."

He told them about his experience with the farmer.

"There's one farmer that won't have much trouble getting along in the world," he said. "He's a hired man now, but I'll bet he'll end up as a con man in some racket in New York before he dies."

Everyone laughed.

"Did you find who leased the pier?" asked Shakespeare.

"No," said King. "No one has leased that pier. I went to a real estate office and they found out for me that the pier has been condemned for two years."

"It looked to me as if it was liable to fall down any minute," said the Key.

King shot a glance at him. "Say," he said. "That reminds me. I wonder if that board that the gold alligator chewed in two was rotten like the building."

"What board that what alligator chewed through?" the Key demanded.

"Oh, that's right," said King. "I didn't tell you about it."

He told them then.

The Bishop shuddered.

"From what I saw of that alligator and his swallowing that giant negro," he said, "I don't think I'd need any demonstration of his powerful jaws."

"Yeah," King said. "But there might be something to that just the same. You know I can't help but think there's something awful fishy about that golden alligator—and I don't care how natural he looks."

"What do you mean?" the Key asked.

"I don't know," King replied. Then he went on eating.

159

A few minutes later King finished and pushed back his plate.

"Of course, the idea of his being all gold—that's crazy to begin with. An alligator was never born that color. Two or three coats of gilt paint would fix that part of it up. That's easy to explain.

"But the other part of it. I'm not so sure about that. I guess it's just the fact that I've never heard of a trained alligator—at least, an alligator that you could train as well as you could a horse or a dog. Anyway, we're shoving off for Florida right now if everybody's ready. And I have a hunch—"

HE STOPPED short. Suddenly a humming sound had come out of the short wave radio receiver on the table. Then a voice was filling the room.

"Hello, Secret 6. Hello, Secret 6. This is Legs Larkin talking. I got a message from the Dummy. I met him and he wasn't going home yet. So I told him I'd deliver it.

"The Dummy has got some dope from the police about that cruiser that pulled off that pier last night. They chased it out into the open ocean. But it got away. When they last saw it, it was headed south.

"They didn't get close enough to it to see the name or number on it. Maybe that'll help you some. You got me? This is Legs Larkin signing off."

King nodded significantly.

"You see," he said. "I don't think that gold alligator is through with us yet. Or maybe I should say we're not through with the gold alligator."

"I'm afraid I don't understand," said the Bishop.

"Simply this," said King. "And understand, this is merely a hunch. But unless I'm crazy, that gold alligator and the express cruiser that left the pier last night are hooked up together in some way."

"What?" exploded the Key. "That dam—I mean, darned alligator that swallowed the big black boy who was supposed to be his boss?"

"I'm convinced," said King, "that the negro who took me out of jail is only one of several associates or members or whatever you may call them of this Order of the Golden Alligator.

"And when you're dealing with a trained animal, it is apt to go haywire sometimes. It looks to me as though the 'gator got his signals crossed. He swallowed the big black boy instead of me."

"But surely," said Shakespeare, "you don't expect to see this gold alligator in Florida?"

"If I don't," said King, "I'll be very much surprised. Let's go. Everybody ready?"

## CHAPTER 11
## EVERGLADES CITY

THE FIVE remaining members of the Secret 6 moved to the door with what personal effects and baggage they were taking. It wasn't much—tooth brushes, razors and a sun helmet or two.

The Bishop's eyes sparkled as he picked up his collapsible deep-sea fishing rod.

"When possible," he said, "I always believe in mixing pleasure with business. I've read quite a bit about Everglades City. There's some tarpon fishing down there. You know, to me, hooking a real big tarpon would be almost as good as finding that hundred million dollars in gold."

They were walking through the woods toward the long narrow flying field that King had developed for his private use.

"Holy gee!" the Key moaned, "I can't figure the kind of stuff that gives you guys a good time. Trading an interest in a hundred million bucks for a mess of fish!"

"In other words," the Bishop chuckled, "you wouldn't sell your birthright for a mess of fish. Is that it, Key?"

"Well, yeah," said the Key. "Something like that."

"I'm afraid," said the Bishop, "you'll never get the proper outlook on things, Key. After all, money is only something that you can buy other things with."

"Sure," said the Key. "But don't think I wouldn't have a good time. If I had a hunk of that million I wouldn't figure to swap much of it for a fish."

"I don't imagine," King said, "that you're going to get much of a hunk of the hundred million."

"What would you do with it?" asked the Bishop.

"What would I do with it?" exploded the Key. "Say, listen. With a hunk of that million I'd make little old New York sit up and take notice. I'd have me thirty-five suits of clothes like the champ. And I'd have all kinds of automobiles. And I'd have yachts."

"What would you do with them all?" asked King. "You couldn't use more than one at a time. As it is, you've got a big roadster and a fast-stepping sedan at your disposal, besides a cruiser that's a good comfortable little craft."

"Yes," added the Bishop. "And we have a roof over our heads and plenty to eat. We manage to find enough to buy proper clothing. And we have each other as friends. There's little more than that to get out of life. Besides, we have the satisfaction of knowing that we're of real service to humanity in this crusade against crime."

They had reached the side of the plane under the trees.

"Well, anyway," said the Key, rather at a loss for further argument, "I'll bet I could have a lot of fun with a hunk of that dough."

"I'll bet," said King, "you wouldn't have as much fun with it as we're having trying to save it for Hernando. From the looks of things, he and his daughter are about as close to its rightful owners as anyone I know."

King unlocked the door and opened it. He entered first, since he had to climb to one of the pilot's seats in front.

"Go easy," he said. "Remember Hernando's body is here in the aisle."

"Think I could forget that?" asked the Key. "This is sure going to be a happy excursion. I can tell that right now. Special rates to Florida with a stiff aboard!"

"There is some superstition about that," said Shakespeare. "Now that I come to think about it. There was a play written around that idea some time ago."

"What idea do you mean?" asked King.

"There seems to be a superstition," said Shakespeare, "among crews of ships, if the vessel is carrying a corpse or there are cripples on board who walk with crutches, that a rough voyage is due."

"I don't know of any cripples," said King. "But superstitions never bothered me very much. Everybody ready?"

Heads nodded.

"Okay," he said. "Here she goes."

The great engine blasted out in a deafening roar. The plane grew light, lifted and climbed above the trees. King banked around and headed south.

HE REACHED up over his head. Pulled a lever that cut in the muffler. They roared along at high speed. He flew across Long Island in the space of a few minutes and went soaring out over the open sea.

"I don't suppose," King ventured to the Key who was sitting in the co-pilot's seat, "that we'd have a chance of picking up that express cruiser on its way south."

"You might," said the Key. "If you knew what to look for."

"Only trouble is, there's plenty of cruisers heading south about now and I haven't any idea what it looks like."

King grew more thoughtful.

"Anyhow," he said, "I think we'll follow the inland canals all the way down."

"What are you going to do if you do find it?" asked the Key.

King shook his head. "I'll be blessed if I know. We're following the coastal route. It'll be a little safer than flying inland because we've got our pontoons to use when we lift the wheels if we have to."

They were flying at five thousand feet now. The south shore had drifted from them so that it was a dim line against the northern horizon. At the left there was nothing but the open sea.

Ahead and to the right the south Jersey coast began to come in view. King veered off, kept out to sea a little, and droned on.

An hour later the Key said, "I thought we were going to follow the inland canals."

King smiled at him.

"Maybe you weren't out there to see that express cruiser get under way," he said. "That's one of the fastest boats I've ever seen—that is, for a cruiser. I'll bet she can make forty-five or fifty knots, if she can make one. And at that rate it isn't going to take her long to get down there.

"She got started last night. She's been going about sixteen or eighteen hours. That means she's way on down the coast now a good deal farther than we are. I wouldn't be surprised if we didn't do much more than catch up with her by this evening."

As time went on he swung closer to the shore. Roared over the Virginia capes and down the coast of North Carolina.

The sun was getting lower and lower in the west.

Several times King dropped low over the point in the coast where small crafts were forced to take to the open sea because of the absence of inland waterways. They spotted small crafts moving southward and dived down to get a better look at them.

Most of them were fishing cruisers. Three, they saw, were keeping a course to the south—wealthy folks following the path of the migratory birds to the tropics.

"None of those," the Key said, "looks as if it could make forty-five or fifty miles an hour."

Suddenly he sat up straight. The ocean had been like a mill pond all the way down. Scarcely a ripple and not even a ground swell could be seen from the air.

But King's eyes were staring far ahead. He reached for a powerful pair of glasses, adjusted them, and peered at the tiny speck. He smiled.

"I think we've spotted it—or a craft very much like it. At least we've got a very fast express cruiser before us. And they're making mighty good time for open sea. Look at the V of spray they're kicking up."

"Jolly!" said the Bishop. "I can see something down there but not quite that much."

"Here, take these glasses," King said, handing them over his shoulder.

The Bishop took them and exclaimed, "They're making time all right!"

"At that rate," said King, "they'll be down there in not much over another day."

"You mean to Everglades City?" asked the Bishop.

"Yes," said King.

"I think you're a bit optimistic," said the Bishop. "They're making excellent time, I'll grant you. But don't forget they can't cut across Florida as we can. They'll have to go a hundred or a hundred-and-fifty miles south of Miami before they can pass through the keys. Then, after that, they'll have to cut up the west coast."

"I guess you're right," said King. "I'd forgot they couldn't cut across land. I'm afraid I wouldn't make much of a boat pilot."

"Well," said the Key, "what are we sitting up here for? Why don't you dive on them so we can get a better look. Gee! If we only had a bomb!"

"Then what?" asked King.

THE KEY looked at him in surprise. "Why, just drop it, that's all. Blow the whole thing up. You'd end all this business about the gold alligator, wouldn't you?"

"If we were sure that was the craft we were looking for," King said, "we probably would. As it stands now, that cruiser down there is just one of the fast express boats. There are a great many of them all over the United States. And from a distance they all look alike. That might be, for instance, the boat of John Astor-bilt."

"Yeah. Or Mr. Waldorf Astoria," the Key cut in. "But aren't you going down there for a look at them?"

King shook his head. "I don't think that would help any," he said. "I'm reasonably sure that that's the cruiser that we're after. But even if it is, there's no use making them suspicious by tearing down and circling their boat."

While he was talking he was losing altitude gradually.

The crimson ship of the Secret 6 was down to an altitude of a thousand feet, then five hundred. King turned and spoke over his shoulder to the Bishop.

"Try to watch that cruiser as we pass it. See if you can see anyone who might be easily described. And try not to let them see that you're watching them."

"Very well," said the Bishop. They were passing the cruiser now.

"I can't see anything but a man in a sailor cap at the wheel," the Bishop declared.

They swept on down the coast and as the sun was setting, they saw the quaint old city of Charleston just ahead down the coast.

"I think we may as well land here. We've got to gas up before we reach Everglades City and we can get something to eat, too," King remarked.

"I think that's an excellent idea," said the Bishop.

He pulled up the wheels dropped the pontoons and landed in Charleston harbor. They found a gas barge, had their tanks filled and then taxied to a public wharf where they tied up for the night.

King locked the door, leaving the corpse of John Hernando inside.

Shakespeare, the Bishop, the Key and King registered at a hotel. Luga went for the night to the colored section of the city.

It was a little past midnight when King was aroused from his sleep by the jangling of the telephone.

The clerk at the desk said, "Your black man is down here and wants to see you. He's very much excited about something."

King dressed hurriedly and went down. He found Luga waiting in the hotel entrance.

"Master," said Luga. "Luga think maybe better go see ship little while ago before going to bed. I go down very quiet. Find two men beside it. Can't see very good. Very dark.

"Hear men hammer. Luga run for them. They see me. They

shoot. Then they run to boat beside our plane before I can catch them. Boat go off in big hurry. Luga think they do some damage to engine. Come and tell you."

"Fine," said King. "Come on. Let's hurry."

They stepped into a taxi outside a hotel and rattled down the narrow street of Charleston to the place where the plane was tied.

King turned a flashlight on the craft. Stared at the engine.

"I should say they have done something to the engine!" he exclaimed. "They've pounded one cylinder almost completely off and they've battered a couple of valve mechanisms so they'll never work again. I suppose they thought they'd tie us up here so they could beat us to Everglades City."

"That the cruiser we look for all right," said Luga.

"You bet it is," said King. "We'll sure look for it this time. Maybe you'd better stay here for the rest of the night."

"Yes," said the faithful black. "Luga was going to."

"Maybe you can catch some sleep on the dock beside the plane. This is going to be a ticklish job, getting the engine repaired with the corpse inside the cabin. I'm afraid Hernando is going to make himself evident before long—the body hasn't been embalmed."

King hurried back to the hotel. After a long time he was talking to the manager of the Charleston airport. Fortunately, there were parts for his motor that could be taken from another not in use.

"I'll meet you at the airport," King said. "In a half hour. No,

171

you won't need a mechanic. I'll do the work myself. I'd rather have it that way."

**BY THREE** o'clock that morning he had the parts needed and was back working on his engine. By five o'clock he had the engine in working condition again. He went back to breakfast and found the Key, the Bishop and Shakespeare up and dressed and wondering where their leader was. He told them what had happened.

"You aren't going to hesitate now about dropping a bomb on them?" the Key asked. "Are you?"

King was tight-lipped.

"No," he said. "But I don't know where to get any bombs. Perhaps a case of dynamite dropped from three hundred feet would do the trick."

He learned of a store that was open early where he could buy dynamite and procured a case.

It was a little past 7 o'clock when they reached the plane. King stored the box of dynamite away between the two front seats.

"I hope," said Shakespeare, "that we don't crash with this load of explosives on board."

King grinned over his shoulder.

"If we do," he said, "it won't make much difference."

He started the engine. It ran smoothly as it had when he tested it. When it was warm they took off in the water and headed south.

"Unless I'm crazy that express cruiser is going to get it," he mused.

Eyes stared as they swept down the coast. He studied the

map. Found where the inland waterway ran down the coast of Florida through the Indian River.

"I think," he said, "we'd better follow that. It'll probably be the course the cruiser will take."

They plowed on down, keeping careful watch for the express boat. But it didn't come in sight. King shook his head in disgust.

"Either they went far out into the ocean or else they tied up somewhere and we missed them. Perhaps it made faster time since midnight than we thought it did."

"We must be almost to Miami," ventured Shakespeare, "according to the map."

"Yes," said King. "I think that little town below us there with the streets laid out like a great city and very few houses on them is Hollywood."

"Holy gee!" said the Key. "Let's take a look at some of the movie stars."

King laughed. "I don't think you'll find them here," he said. "This is Hollywood, Florida. That's Miami in the distance. Now, according to the map, if we'd swing over to the right we could follow the Tamiami Trail to Everglades City."

They droned on for perhaps twenty minutes. The southwest coast of Florida came into view and they saw the little settlement of houses that was the first of Everglades City.

"Holy gee!" shouted the Key. "Look at those islands."

"Yes," said King. "Ten thousand of them. Count them if you don't believe it."

They saw a winding canal leading from the center of the settlement out into the water that surrounded the countless islands. King swung around, cut his motor and landed the plane near the mouth of the canal.

He turned and began taxiing up the canal slowly. For it was quite narrow in places and the wings threatened to touch the sides.

They had gone perhaps halfway through the canal when they rounded a turn and came face-to-face with a medium-sized cabin cruiser plowing slowly toward the islands.

There was a young woman perched on the upper deck of the cruiser. She was dressed in a pair of white ducks with a man's white shirt open at the throat. Her dark eyes flashed for a moment. Her black hair waved in the breeze.

The only other occupant of the cruiser was dark also. Slightly dark, like the girl. There was a similarity in their faces.

On the bow the King saw the name of the craft in gold letters, *Owassa.*

## CHAPTER 12
## JOHN OGDEN

I N THAT first moment the girl's eyes flashed. She called out to them. "Ship ahoy. Hold it. We can't pass in this canal."

King was half up in his seat, head and shoulders out of a side window. He felt almost as though he knew this man and the girl with the dark eyes and hair.

The two not only resembled each other very strikingly, but they also bore a strong likeness to John Hernando, the young man whose body now lay in the aisle of the low-winged speed-plane. It was as clear to King as though someone had been there to introduce them to him.

King called out to the girl in answer.

"If I'm guessing right we won't have to pass in this canal."

He saw the lovely, dark eyes of the girl look perplexed. There was a glint of fear there too—or was it mere uncertainty? King hastened to reassure her.

"Your name is Hernando, isn't it?"

Both crafts had stopped and were drifting a little closer together. King turned his motor so they could talk more easily as the man left the wheel of the cruiser. The girl had nodded in answer to King's question. The man leaned over the side of the cruiser.

"I'm John Hernando," he said. "What's wanted?"

He had the appearance of a kind, fatherly man, past fifty, but he had a look of worry on his face—a look, King thought at first glance, of almost perpetual worry. King hesitated.

It was hard to break the news, and he wanted to do it as gently as possible.

"We just flew down from New York to see you," King called across the short space of water.

A look of deep concern flashed across the face of young Hernando's uncle. His eyes had taken in the other members of the Secret 6 who were in the ship. He could see them through the cabin windows. King noted the look of anxiety. There was suspicion in the dark eyes of the girl.

"Don't worry," said King. "We've come down to help."

"Is anything wrong?" asked the man anxiously.

"I'll tell you about everything when we can find a place where we can talk alone," he said. "I don't want to shout all the information I have out here in the open. But you can rest assured of one thing.

"You'll understand when I tell you who we are. We've come down to give you what help we can. We have no idea of personal gain. You can count on us absolutely as friends."

The worried look on the man's face subsided a little. He nodded resignedly.

"Very well," he said. "I'll turn around and you can follow me back. Or would you like to have me tow you?"

"Perhaps that would be better," said King. "Throw me a line, if you have one. This ship's pretty difficult to handle in a narrow canal."

"Yes," said Hernando.

King turned to Luga.

"Climb out on the pontoon, will you, Luga?" he asked. "And catch the line and make it fast."

"Yes, master," said Luga.

He saw the girl and her father both stare at the giant Zulu chief as he climbed out on the pontoon and waited for the line to be thrown. King didn't stop to explain Luga.

"All right," he called. "Let's have the rope."

The girl showed her ability as a capable seaman. She perched easily on the bow of the deck with the coiled rope in her hands, held one end of it in her left and threw it with her right.

The coil wriggled out across the water. Luga caught it and

tied it to one of the brace members. The girl walked lightly to the stern of the cruiser. There she fastened the line.

"All right?" asked Hernando.

"Okay," said King. "Tow away."

The engine of the cruiser which had been throttled now rumbled a little harder. The craft was turning. They moved on slowly down the winding canal.

About half a mile beyond they came to the settlement that was known as Everglades City and pulled into the docks. Several people stared curiously at the great crimson, low-winged monoplane.

There were other small charter cruisers tied to the dock that ran lengthwise of the canal.

King hopped out of the seat and started back, stepping gingerly over the stiff corpse. He stepped to the pontoon and then to the dock. The others followed. The man of God with the twinkling eyes spoke to King in a low voice before Hernando and his daughter had left their craft.

"Do you want us to bring the body out now?" he asked.

"I don't think so," said King. "Not yet. I'm afraid that'd be pretty much of a shock. Let's wait until we've had a chance to explain the whole thing to them and then perhaps it would be better to have the local undertaker, if they have one down here, take care of it."

HERNANDO AND his daughter were advancing down the dock while King made the plane fast.

"Perhaps it would be best," said Hernando, "if we go to my

home and we can talk in privacy. It's only a block or so from here."

He glanced significantly at the throng of townspeople who had collected about the place.

"Yes," said King. "I'll try to explain everything then."

He and the four members of the Secret 6 were on the dock now. King walked back along the pontoon and locked the cabin door of the ship.

Then, with Hernando and his daughter leading, they walked out past a little parkway, turned left and a block beyond entered a low one-story frame bungalow.

"We aren't used to having so many people here at once. But I think we can all find seats," Hernando said.

When they were seated, King began.

"Mr. Hernando, I may as well make this as brief as possible. But I want to tell you enough so you'll understand everything. Naturally, no one is more interested in what I'm going to tell you than you are.

"To begin with I'll introduce myself. Have you ever heard of the Secret 6?"

The girl moved a little nearer the edge of her chair. Hernando hesitated for a moment. Frowned.

"Why, yes," said the girl. "We've heard of the Secret 6. Don't you remember, father, I was reading something about the Secret 6 in the paper—some case they'd been on. Don't you remember about the giant?"

"I remember," said Hernando.

King smiled a little. "I think," he said, "we can safely trust you and your daughter, Mr. Hernando. You see, we are five members of the Secret 6."

The girl gasped.

"I'm King," he said. "This is the Bishop, and Shakespeare there, and the Key. This is Luga sitting next to me."

They all rose as their names were mentioned and bowed to the girl. Instantly all fear and suspicion seemed to leave Hernando and his daughter.

"I—" he said. "I can hardly believe it. Why, I couldn't have wished anything more perfect than you gentlemen entering the case. I have told you, of course, who I am. And this is my daughter, Inez."

The men bowed again and sat down.

"I hope," Hernando went on, looking anxious again, "that nothing is wrong. But I'm afraid something has turned up or five of you wouldn't have taken the trouble to come down here."

"All six of us will be here probably this afternoon," said King. "The Doctor prefers to travel by train. He should be arriving in Miami about noon or shortly after. Then he will hire a car and come out."

King cleared his throat. Hernando simply nodded and waited for him to go on.

"I met your nephew," King said, "in New York." He hesitated, but finally got underway and began the story with considerable detail.

Hernando and his daughter were horrified. King tried to be as gentle as he could in breaking the news. But the facts were there and they had to be told.

He told them of the organization of the Golden Alligator; of the attack of the golden alligator and of his swallowing the negro.

Inez shuddered.

Her father spoke with a choked voice. "What happened to John's body?" he asked.

"We brought it down with us in the plane," King said. "But I wanted to explain things first before I told you about that. I think probably it would be best if you just turned the body over to your local undertaker."

Hernando glanced at his daughter. She wasn't sobbing. She was trying to control herself and her mouth was set in a grim straight line of determination. Hernando nodded.

"Have you an undertaker in Everglades City?" asked King.

Hernando nodded again. Found words a moment later.

"He's the man who runs the furniture and hardware store down in the block beside the hotel."

"Then," King said, "I think we'd better go down and take care of that end of it. We'll leave you and your daughter until this afternoon."

HE GLANCED significantly at the others of the Secret 6 there in the room. They rose silently and followed him out.

Hernando came to the door. "I can't express my gratitude to you gentlemen," he said.

King was about to say, "It's a pleasure, Mr. Hernando." Then he checked himself. That wasn't quite the thing to say in a case like this.

Instead he said, "Perhaps it would be just as well if you wouldn't mention our identity to anyone."

"Of course not," said Hernando. Then he closed the door. King shook his head as he walked down the street toward the hardware and undertaking establishment.

"Mighty tough for the girl," he said. "And Hernando, too, for that matter. I imagine the young fellow has been more like a son and brother to them than a nephew and cousin since his father was killed."

They arranged to have the body of young Hernando removed from the plane to the undertaking establishment.

"I suppose," said King to the undertaker, "the local police will have to be mixed up in this."

The undertaker was very curious.

"Sure," he said. "Why not? What killed young John, anyway? Too bad. He was a right nice boy."

"He seemed so," said King, "young Hernando was—"

King stopped suddenly.

"By the way. I just happened to think of something that I want to see his uncle about. If you'll excuse me I'll run over a moment."

He rapped gently on the front door of the little bungalow where the Hernandos lived. Hernando answered. Opened the door.

"I'm sorry to bother you so soon again," King said. "But a matter just came up. I suppose you know the undertaker very well. And the police?"

"I should say so," said Hernando. "I was brought up with both of them. I went to school with them. The deputy sheriff here is one of my best friends."

"I don't think," said King, "It would be very well to risk letting this thing get farther than Everglades City. If the police—say, in Miami—learn about us bringing the body down from New York, without notifying any authorities up there, there's pretty apt to be an investigation. I'm afraid we don't want that just now. These friends of yours, the deputy sheriff and the undertaker, know about your secret of the buried treasure?"

Hernando shook his head. "No," he said. "Nothing's ever been said down here about that. We've kept that in the family. I wouldn't dare let it out. Especially down here. We'd have the whole of Miami to say nothing of the United States, down in the Ten Thousand Islands digging them all up if it ever got around."

King was thoughtful for a moment. "That's not so good," he said. "We can't very well come out and tell exactly what happened to your nephew. Do you know your local doctor down here?"

"Very well," said Hernando.

"He'll probably have to examine the body."

"Yes."

"Suppose I cook up a story about getting his neck caught on a wire. I'll tell them we're friends of yours. We've been down on fishing parties before. And that he was with us when the accident happened. And we brought his body directly down here."

Hernando hesitated.

"I think maybe I'd better go with you. They'd believe me, anyway."

By the time King and Hernando reached the undertaking

establishment the undertaker had gotten both the local examining physician and the deputy sheriff there. Hernando nodded gravely to them.

"Boys," he said, "this is a very good friend of mine. Mr. King. He was with my nephew when he was accidentally killed. It was at night, wasn't it, Mr. King?"

King nodded.

"Yes. We were taking a walk. Talking over the old fishing days down here. I was on the street side. John was on the other side. It was in the suburbs of Long Island near Flushing.

"He stepped on the outside of the sidewalk in the dark. Suddenly I realized he'd vanished from beside me where he'd been a moment before. I heard a choking sound. Then, too late, I found his body below the sidewalk.

"There was a steep gorge at the side. When we looked over the ground in the morning we found that the sidewalk had given way under him. We'd had a lot of rain up there. John had slipped and fell. And in the darkness a fence wire had caught around his neck and hung him.

"We thought it would be much better to bring him directly down here by plane, but we've been two days in coming. We've had a lot of motor trouble."

The local doctor nodded.

"I was just going to ask you that," he said. "Young John seems to have been dead about two days."

"I think that answers your question," said King. "Of course, we'd have been down in nine or ten hours if it hadn't been for the motor trouble."

He glanced at the deputy sheriff and the undertaker. They seemed to believe him.

"Too bad," said the sheriff. "John was a nice boy."

The elder Hernando spoke in a husky voice. "We'll leave matters with you," he told the undertaker. "I think we'd better have the funeral here in the back rooms. Just a quiet affair with only the friends and family."

"When do you want it to be, John?" asked the undertaker.

"Say, tomorrow afternoon?" said Hernando. "Would that be too soon?"

He glanced at King. "Would tomorrow morning be all right?" King asked. "My friends and I would like to be here at his funeral and we have some things we have to take care of in the afternoon."

"Tomorrow morning," said the elder Hernando.

"All right," said the undertaker. "I'll have everything ready."

There was one hotel in the place. That was just back of the business block. King and his band registered there. It was a typical sportsman's resort hotel.

All about the lobby were trophies of fishing trips. Sharks' jaws. A great tarpon mounted on a board. The silver fins of tarpons, large and small, varying in sizes.

They had lunch, walked about the main corner of the wharf.

"Well," said King, about the middle of the afternoon, "The Doctor ought to be here shortly. I don't imagine there'll be much going on until after the funeral is over tomorrow. Hernando and his daughter have enough to worry about without us talking to them now."

It was half an hour later that a car swung down the main street. The car had the appearance of being a taxi.

"Hey!" the Key jerked. "There's the Doctor sitting in the back seat of that car."

King stared. Then he stiffened. "Who's that beside him?" he demanded.

The car swung a little nearer so that now King could get a good view of the man on the other side of the Doctor. Neither of the men in the car had seen them.

"Say!" the Key hissed. "That's the guy you sent me out to shadow."

King's eyes almost popped out of his head.

"By George! It is!" he exploded. "There's the Doctor in the back seat of that car. And that's Ogden—John L. Ogden—sitting beside him!"

## CHAPTER 13
## OGDEN ALIAS SMITH

ALL FIVE of the Secret 6 were staring at the car as it swung by the little parkway where they had stopped and drew up before the hotel.

"That's the guy," the Key said. "Ogden. He's the guilty one. Now, let's nail him!"

But King caught him by the arm and held him back. "Take it easy. After all, the mere fact that he came down here on the train with the Doctor isn't any evidence that he's the man we're after. We've got to wait until we get more dope than that on him. And I don't think it'll be long."

"You mean you're going to let him walk right out of your fingers?" demanded the Key.

King shook his head. "No, he'll be watched. But we don't want to let him know it. Bishop, he doesn't know you and Shakespeare. Suppose you two keep tabs on him. Watch his room. Shadow him wherever he goes. If he hires a cruiser and goes on a supposed fishing party, hire another and trail him."

"But how can he be the guilty one?" asked the Bishop. "He couldn't have gotten down here in this short time in that express cruiser."

"I did think," replied King, "that the man we're after was coming down on that express cruiser. But he might have sent the cruiser down with its crew and traveled on the train."

"Then what good would the cruiser be?" inquired the Key.

"Among the Ten Thousand Islands," the Bishop said, "they would, no doubt, find a use for it."

"Let's talk to the Doctor when we can get him alone," King said, "and see what he's found out. The Key, Luga and I will hang around the docks while you two go in to the hotel.

"Remember, now. Keep an eye on Ogden constantly. Don't let him out of your sight unless he's in his room."

The Bishop and Shakespeare departed for the hotel. King spoke in a parting shout, "You might tell the Doctor when he's at liberty to come out and meet us here."

Then he, Luga and the Key walked to the long dock that skirted the end of the canal and sauntered about aimlessly. It was some time later that King saw the Doctor leave the door of the hotel and come toward them. He had a puzzled expression on his face when he reached them.

"What's this all about?" he demanded. "I couldn't get anything out of Shakespeare and the Bishop except that you were waiting over here for me."

"You mean," King asked, "that you haven't any idea whom you rode up with?"

"Sure," said the Doctor. "Some fellow from New York by the name of Smith. Not a particularly pleasant chap.

"But not bad. He said he ran down here for a few days' rest."

King smiled a little. "Listen, Doctor," he said, "I've been here a few hours longer than you have. Ordinarily, people don't come to Everglades City for a rest. They come to fish. Of course, you can call that a change and a rest, if you want to. And another thing. His name isn't Smith. At least, if his name is Smith, the name he gave young John Hernando wasn't correct."

"What?" exclaimed the Doctor. "You mean he's one of the—"

King nodded.

"Yes. One of the six honest men who answered Hernando's ad. According to the list that Hernando left that's John L. Ogden. He's supposed to be a merchant. Does he look like a merchant to you, Doctor? Does he talk like one?"

"I should say not," the Doctor said. "He acts more like a gambler or racketeer. Although he doesn't seem like a bad sort. Oh, you've got Shakespeare and the Bishop in there watching him, have you?"

"Yes," said King. "They're going to shadow him everywhere he goes." His eyes narrowed. "I think, Doctor, we've got our man."

"Well, what are you waiting for then?" asked the Doctor. "Let's go nab this Ogden—or Smith or whatever his name is—and put him through third degree. We'll get it out of him."

"No, I think there's an easier way," said King. "Did he say anything to you about buried treasure or gold alligators on the trip down?"

THE DOCTOR chuckled. "Far from it," he said. "Smith—or Ogden—was talking politics mostly. New York City politics. I guess he must have recognized me on the way down on the train. We were in the same car together. Then when we got off at the station in Miami we both headed for the nearest cab.

"I blurted out something about going to Everglades City and Ogden said he was going to the same place. And we'd ride together. We'd split the taxi fare if that was all right with me. And so I said, 'Yes!'

"To tell you the truth I don't remember much of what he did say. New York politics have never been much of a hobby with me."

King stared thoughtfully across at the hotel entrance almost hidden by the growth of strange tropical trees and the little park between.

"So he was talking about New York politics," he said half to himself. "Well, he's a good bluffer, anyway. And his name is Smith! That's a good one."

He stopped for a moment.

"Look," he said. "There he is now. I can just see him on the sidewalk. Cigar in one corner of his mouth. He's out seeing the town."

"Yeah," said the Key. "And there's the Bishop and Shakespeare behind him."

At least King and the Key, who had met Ogden before in the room, kept as much out of sight as they could for the rest of the afternoon. Now and then they received reports from either the Bishop or Shakespeare.

"I tell you what you do, Doctor," said King late that afternoon. "Get hold of him tonight. Feel him out. Maybe get him in a game of pinochle or something. He looks like the pinochle type.

"Although he might be able to take you over for a game of poker. Use your own judgment about that. But feel him out."

King and the Key went to the dining room early that evening. They took a table in one far corner. They sat with their backs to the entrance so that Ogden could not see them when he came in.

They left before most of the others had finished. Ogden wasn't in sight when they went out again. They walked outside through the warm tropical evening. Shakespeare came behind them.

As he passed he said, "Follow me around the corner. I have something to tell you."

There they stopped at the edge of a playground where they heard a dozen or so monkeys chattering.

"A strange thing has happened," Shakespeare told them when they were alone. "Ogden went into the dining room a short time ago. He went in rather late for dinner. The Bishop was with the Doctor. Ogden went into the dining room and glanced around. He seemed to be looking for someone.

"Then he went out again. He's just gone into the dining room now. Went in a couple of minutes after you came out. The Bishop was watching then. He just told me to tell you."

King lighted a cigarette.

"I wonder," he said, "who he was looking for? I'd give a lot to know."

That night King and the Key, keeping in the background, saw the Doctor and Ogden together.

"It's working," King said. "Let's get out of the way and let the Doctor handle it for tonight. I wonder how soon that express cruiser will be down."

He did a bit of mental calculating.

"It surely ought to be here by tomorrow night. And I think by then things will start humming."

But in the morning a conference with the Doctor disclosed nothing.

At ten o'clock the funeral of young John Hernando was held. King represented the Secret 6. The rest of them stayed away. The Doctor was again with Ogden.

A little before noon, when the funeral was over, he had nothing to report.

"That fellow is as tight as a clam," he said. "I can't get a thing out of him. I've made suggestions of alligators and the possibility of pirates having buried treasure down in this country. And while he's lively enough in talking about other subjects, he doesn't seem to be a bit interested in that line of conversation."

"He'll be before long," King said. "I think he's probably heard about the funeral of Hernando."

King stared harder as he saw someone move at the window.

"What do you mean?" asked the Doctor.

"Well, if I've got the thing straight," King said, "we'll find Ogden hooking up with Hernando very shortly. At least you'll find him making a call upon him. Suppose you keep an eye on Hernando's house and let me know what you see."

In a half hour the Doctor reported hack.

"By George!" he said. "You were right. Partially. Ogden has been taking a walk for the last half hour so he could be in constant sight of Hernando's bungalow."

"Didn't he go in?" asked King.

"No," said the Doctor. "That's the funniest part of it. He seems to be waiting and watching for someone."

They rounded a corner and stood in the shelter of a group of palms. The Doctor pointed.

"See. There he is. Two blocks away now. He's walking in the opposite direction. But every now and then he turns and looks back at the Hernando bungalow."

King frowned.

"And come to think about it," said the Doctor. "I was with him almost all morning walking around the town. I hadn't thought of it before, but it seems to me we were almost always in sight of that bungalow."

SUDDENLY KING tensed as they stood there. A car had stopped down the street. Stopped near a pedestrian on the sidewalk. From a distance it looked like another private car used for taxi work such as the Doctor and Ogden had come in from Miami.

The pedestrian was now pointing out the bungalow of the Hernandos. Then the car drove on.

It stopped in front of the Hernando house. A man was getting out of the car. A tall, distinguished-looking gentleman. He said something to the driver. Then he went up and rang the door bell. They saw him standing out in front for perhaps a full minute.

The door opened and they could see Hernando talking to him. Another minute and they saw the man who had arrived in the car go in.

King shot a glance at Ogden. He had stopped under the overhanging fronds of a cocoanut palm down the street and across it. He was watching. Watching the Hernando bungalow. The door closed behind the newcomer.

King took a long breath.

"If that doesn't complicate things," he said, "I don't know what does."

"What do you mean?" asked the Doctor.

"You wouldn't know who that man was at Hernando's house, would you?"

The Doctor shook his head.

"That's another one of the six honest men," King said. "We have two of them in town now."

"Who is it?" the Doctor asked.

"Freeman," said King. "Clinton J. Freeman. He's the headmaster of the school that has winter quarters near St. Petersburg."

"But I thought you said you would trust him sooner than any of the rest of the six honest men."

"I did," said King.

"Then what's he doing down here?" asked the Doctor.

"That's what we're going to find out just as soon as he leaves the house," King said. "You better not be seen with me the rest of the afternoon. I don't want Ogden to know that you and I have any connection."

"What do you want me to do?" asked the Doctor.

"Just take it easy and keep out of sight," King replied.

The Doctor left then.

King stayed behind the palms. Now and then he glanced at Ogden and then again at the house where Clinton J. Freeman had entered. He stood where he could get a good view of the bungalow. Faced the front of it.

He stared a little harder through the palms as he saw something move at the window. A curtain was drawn back and for a brief moment he saw Freeman's face at the window.

"That's funny," he said. "I wonder what's up now."

But he waited almost a half hour. Learned nothing more at the end of that time except that Freeman came out of the house. Got in his car and was driven to the hotel.

Ogden was coming that way now. King turned abruptly. He tried to keep the palms that sheltered him between Ogden and himself. He went over toward the docks. Crossed the little park. Didn't think Ogden had noticed him. He certainly hoped he hadn't.

Ogden turned the corner and went toward the hotel. When Ogden went inside, King walked rapidly to the Hernando bungalow. In answer to his ring, Hernando came to the door. He was grave-faced and sad.

"I just had a caller," he said. "In regard to the treasure."

"Yes," said King. "I was watching. So was someone else. Who did this man say he was?" King asked.

"He gave his name as—let me see," said Hernando. He took a card from the table. "Clinton J. Freeman. Yes. That was his name."

"That's right," said King. "That is his name. What's he doing down here?"

"Why," said Hernando. "He explained that he was one of the men who answered my nephew's ad. He gave the facts of the case just as you gave them, King. He said he understood that Close was dead and therefore couldn't enter into the deal of finding the treasure with me as my nephew had planned.

"So he thought since my nephew had selected him in the first place, before he had found Close, that I might be glad to take up the matter with him."

"What did you tell him?" asked King.

"Well, naturally," Hernando said, "I told him I'd have to think it over. I wanted to talk it over with you."

"That's mighty nice of you," King said. "I'm glad you didn't give him any definite answer. Another man of the six honest men is down here too," King said.

Hernando's eyes widened.

"What? Already?"

"Yes," said King. "A man who gave his name as John L. Ogden

to your nephew. He's been watching this house all morning. Didn't he come here?"

Hernando shook his head. "I haven't seen anyone else. Of course, there was the—funeral this morning. And after that Inez and I came straight home. The girl was pretty badly shaken. John was like a brother to her.

"I did receive a telegram, however. I told Mr. Freeman about it."

King frowned.

"What telegram?" he asked.

"Here it is," said Hernando, taking the yellow sheet from the table and handing it to King.

King read it swiftly.

It was sent from Jacksonville. It read:

"On my way down to talk over matters I consulted with your nephew. Should arrive sometime late this afternoon. Hold all propositions open until I see you this evening."

It was signed, "W.G. Fuller."

King remembered Fuller, the financier, well. He was big and stern and businesslike. He was the one who had thought his friends were playing a joke on him when someone called up and warned him about the Golden Alligator.

"You've met him, of course?" said Hernando.

"Yes," said King. "He's a financier, I believe. There's one man that looks the part. So he's coming down, too!"

"That makes three of the six you mentioned who answered the ad," said Hernando. "What do you think I should do?"

King spent a minute thinking.

"I don't know," he said. "The way things are developing I don't believe I'd trust anyone with a secret like that. Certainly not at the present time.

"If I were you, I'd just tell everyone I talked with that I had to think the proposition over. Meanwhile, we'll see how things develop and—"

He glanced toward the window. "Say," he said, "didn't I see Freeman get up and look out of the window while he was in here?"

"Er—yes. I believe he did," said Hernando. "As I remember he said something about wanting to see if his car was still waiting."

"Well, I suppose there was nothing wrong in that," King said. He turned for the door. Paused.

"Mr. Hernando," he said, "if I were you I don't believe I'd go out any more than I had to until this thing clears up. Unless you're accompanied by one or two of the Secret 6."

He heard a door open softly at the back of the living room. Inez Hernando came into the room. Her face was white.

Her lips formed a straight, tight line. She wore a dark dress, which complemented her eyes and hair beautifully.

"I heard you say that, Mr. King," she said. "Do you really think Father is in danger?"

King tried to reassure her with a smile.

"I wouldn't go so far as to say that," he said. "However, there's no use of taking any chances until we find out what's going on here. I'll tell you. I'll send Luga over to stay with you constantly. I'm quite sure everything will be all right then."

"Thank you," said the girl, coming a little nearer. "Somehow, I can't help feeling that if you tell me everything is all right, it will be just that way."

"I think it's going to be. But as I said before, there's no use tempting Fate. Soon there'll be three men down here in Everglades City. And each one of them is anxious to get a share, if not all, of that hundred million in gold."

He left then. Sent Luga over to stay at the Hernando bungalow from then on.

It was rather late for lunch when he arrived at the hotel. He glanced ahead cautiously. Scanned the lobby before he came into full view. At that moment neither Ogden nor Freeman was in sight.

King slipped inside. Then everything seemed to be happening at once.

A stocky man came out of the dining room. Puffing a newly lighted cigarette. That was Ogden.

A distinguished looking gentleman came down the stairs, headed for the dining room. That was Clinton J. Freeman.

## CHAPTER 14
## MURDER DIRGE

ALL THREE met unexpectedly in the middle of the lobby. It was too late to turn back. Freeman glanced from Ogden to King and back again to Ogden. He smiled.

"Well, this is a pleasure," he said. "I never dreamed that I'd see you two gentlemen down here."

"Yes," King agreed. "It is a surprise, isn't it?"

He turned to Freeman.

"I suppose you're down here for the fishing?"

For a moment Freeman hesitated. Then he laughed.

"Bless you! No," he said. "This is the time of the year when my entire student body migrates, as it were, to our winter quarters near St. Petersburg. And since they were coming down this way I thought I'd take the opportunity to run down and have a talk with Mr. Hernando on the subject we were all more or less interested in.

"Then, too, I thought it no more than right to pay my respects to him in regards to his nephew's untimely death. I understand his funeral was this morning."

"Yes," said King. "I was there."

Freeman turned abruptly to Ogden.

"I suppose, Mr.—er—Ogden is that the name?"

The other nodded.

"I suppose," Freeman went on, "you're down here for the same reason?"

"No," said Ogden, chewing his cigar. "I can't say that I am. I got curious to see this country Hernando had told me about. Then I needed a rest, anyway. So I just came down to look around."

"Oh," Freeman said, rather taken back. "Then you aren't interested in investing in this proposition of buried—"

"*Shhhh,*" said King. "Not so loud."

"Well," growled Ogden. "Maybe I am and maybe I ain't.

Anyway, it's a nice country. Maybe I'll get in some fishing tomorrow. There's lots of time. I'm just sort of on a vacation."

"And you," said Freeman, turning to King. "I presume you came down to help look after the interests of your friends, the Hernandos? I believe you said they were friends of yours?"

King thought there was a slightly sarcastic tone in his voice. But he evaded that.

"Yes," he said.

"Well, at least," said Freeman, "we're all down here—called, you might say, on the same general mission. Let's have lunch together."

"I've had mine," said Ogden.

"Oh, very well," said Freeman. He turned to King. "Then perhaps you and I?"

"Of course," said King. "Why not?"

But King was left as much in the dark after he had finished his lunch with Freeman as he had been before. He felt as he sat at the table talking aimlessly about this and that with the head-master that he was wasting his time.

He hurried through the meal and excused himself. He wanted to be out watching Ogden. He found him without any trouble, taking his usual walk within sight of the Hernando residence.

Once that afternoon Ogden went to the telephone booth off the lobby and put through a call.

King tried to get near enough to overhear him. But all he could catch was the fact that Ogden was calling New York. The conversation must have been short and low, for King couldn't catch any of that.

Then Ogden resumed his walking.

It was nearly six o'clock when King saw Fuller, the financier, drive up before the Hotel and get out. And through Freeman's apparently genial spirit the four, Ogden, Freeman, King and Fuller, ate dinner together in the dining room that night.

Fuller seemed disgruntled. Out of sorts. He didn't seem to like the idea of these others being down here on the same mission.

King judged from his actions that Hernando had conducted the conference as King had suggested. That Fuller had been told to wait for his decision until Hernando thought the proposition over.

**KING HAD** by this time cut loose from the other members of the Secret 6. Had nothing to do with them. He spent the early hours of the evening sitting in the lobby with the three supposedly honest men.

Several fishermen came in from a late trip among the islands. Then there were stories about the great tarpon and the fights they had put up. Buried treasure seemed forgotten.

Freeman got up finally. Turned to Fuller.

"What do you say to a little walk before we turn in for the night?"

Fuller hesitated. Then he nodded. "Okay with me," he said.

King smiled to himself as he saw the two go off together.

A few minutes later Ogden got up and stretched.

"Well," he said, "I guess I'll have a smoke and then I'll turn in."

King was left alone. He waited perhaps two minutes. Then he, too, went out. Lighted a cigarette. Looked up and down the dimly lighted streets. He had thought he might find and trail Ogden.

He had a feeling that as long as Freeman and Fuller were together nothing particularly serious would happen. Those two at least seemed to be rivals for the same thing.

Perhaps ten minutes had passed. He hadn't found Ogden. Hadn't seen a thing of him.

Then a cry rent the air! A cry from far out along the road that followed the canal for some distance. He thought he recognized the voice.

"Help! Help!" a voice roared out.

Instantly King broke into a dead run. The shouts continued. "Help! Help!"

Out there ahead in the darkness beside the canal he saw a figure running toward him. They met. It was the headmaster of the school.

"What's happened?" King demanded.

"Something terrible," said Freeman. "I'm afraid—Mr. Fuller is dead."

He was panting harder.

"I can't see a thing," Freeman went on, "because I don't happen to have a flashlight and, not being a smoking man, I don't carry matches."

King had a match box out of his pocket before they reached the place where Fuller lay. He struck a light and bent over him. Freeman was on the other side.

King gasped. He saw a glint of gold at Fuller's throat!

Instantly he raised the body to a sitting position. He heard the pounding of feet behind. Others were coming. Frantically King unwound a flying garrote.

It was a gold-plated wire with a golden alligator at each end. A flying garrote exactly like the two that had killed young Hernando and Close.

He succeeded in getting the wire off. Unwound it from around the throat. Of those who were running from the edge of town, the Doctor was first to get there.

"What is it?" he asked.

"Another murder," King said, almost in a whisper.

"Good heavens!" gasped the Doctor. He was feeling for the heart action. "There doesn't seem to be any," he said. "Here. Let me work on him a minute."

He began applying artificial respiration to the choked man. Then suddenly he took something from his pocket.

King was trying to light more matches. In his hurry he had dropped the box and was fumbling for it. He couldn't see what the Doctor was doing.

The Doctor had by now struck a match. A few minutes later he was looking at a thermometer in his hand.

"Hum," he said.

That was all. He straightened and got up.

"I'm sorry," he said, "but I'm afraid the man's past aid."

He turned to King.

"Was there anyone with him when this happened?"

Freeman spoke up.

"Yes," he said. "I was." His voice was a little shaky.

"Tell me just exactly what happened," King said.

"There isn't very much that I know about," said Freeman. "Fuller and I were walking out this road. Suddenly I heard a swishing sound, almost like a soft, throbbing whisper."

King nodded.

"Yes," he said. "That's it."

"Next thing I knew, I couldn't find Fuller. Then I stumbled over his body. He was struggling for a moment. Then he lay still. I remember asking him if he was all right. He didn't answer.

"As I told you before, I don't usually carry matches and I had no flashlight, so couldn't see what had happened. It's not so dark when you're standing but someone on the ground is pretty hard to see out here. Then I called for help. That's all I know."

"I should think," said the Doctor, "that was enough."

King was starting back already. He had taken two or three steps.

"Where are you going?" the Doctor asked, in a low voice.

"To get Ogden," snapped King through tight lips. He started to run, the Doctor just behind.

"Wait!" Freeman pleaded. "Don't leave me here."

"Come on then," growled the Doctor. "You've got legs, haven't you?"

They could hear Freeman coming on now. King and the Doctor came to the paving of the street at the edge of the town. Then a huge form appeared in the dim street lights and was running toward them.

"Master! Master!"

It was Luga.

"Man die!"

They met.

"What are you talking about?" King demanded.

"Stout man die across street from Hernando house. Luga set on front porch. Watch man walk up and down there 'cross road. Then hear sound like whisper over near him. And see him fall. He choke. He dead."

King was racing on.

"Go back to Hernando's," he cried. "Don't leave them alone."

"Yes, master."

Luga was off like a shot again for the Hernando bungalow. King saw him leap up on the porch and open the front door.

THEN KING stumbled and almost fell headlong across a stout body that was lying in the grass between the sidewalk and the street. Across from the Hernando bungalow. King fumbled for a match and lighted it. Stared down.

The sightless eyes of John L. Ogden stared up at him!

"Another one!" ejaculated King.

"Good Lord!" exclaimed the Doctor.

Gold glittered at the throat of Ogden. The gold of the flying garrote.

King was unwinding it swiftly. The Doctor was feeling the pulse of the man.

"Hurry," he said. "There's a chance. There's some life yet."

Then the Doctor was working over the still form of Ogden. Several men came running up. King didn't turn to see who they were. He heard Freeman ask, "What's happened? Someone else—"

"Yes," said King. "Ogden."

King unwound the garrote
as the Doctor felt the
pulse of the fallen man.

"Good heavens!" gasped Freeman.

"Wait," the Doctor said. "He's coming around. This is luck."

Ogden was opening his eyes. He stared and blinked into the sputter of the match that King was holding. He gasped and choked and clutched at his throat.

"I'd like to get the—" he said with difficulty. Then his voice choked up. And he stopped short. Next he was struggling to his feet. He stared around.

"Who choked me?" he demanded, thickly.

"That's what we'd like to know," said King.

"Well," growled Ogden, "if I ever get my hands on that—"

"Do you know who it was or what it was?" asked King.

"No," said Ogden. "I just heard a whispering sound."

"Maybe," said King, "it's about time you told us what you were doing around here."

"Maybe," Ogden retorted. "But I don't think it's any of your business."

"Okay," said King. "Suit yourself. At least I don't think you had anything to do with this last garrote."

"This what?" demanded Ogden.

"Garrote," said King. "The thing that almost killed you. It was the Doctor here who brought you back to life."

Ogden started to walk. But his legs buckled a little. He was weak and shaky.

"Here," King said. "I'll help you. You'd better go back to the hotel and go to bed. And if you know what's good for you, you'd better lock yourself in."

Ogden didn't answer. He let King help him. King took him

to his room. It was one of the front rooms that looked out over the porch roof on the street below. He went outside and closed the door.

"Now, lock the door from the inside," he told Ogden.

"Okay," said Ogden.

King tried the door. It was locked.

King went downstairs to the lobby. There was mad confusion down there. It seemed that everyone in town had heard of the murder and was in the lobby asking questions. People were coming in from the drug store that had an entrance into the lobby.

Two men were carrying the body of Fuller, the financier. As the Doctor had said, he was dead. The local undertaker took charge.

The Bishop and the Key and Shakespeare were asking questions of King. King went to the rear part of the lobby that was raised four or five steps from the lower section. There they stood alone, talking in a group.

There was so much confusion that no one would notice them. And it didn't matter if they did. King had seen Freeman there, repeating his story over and over again as people asked him.

"What's it all about?" asked the Key.

King shrugged.

"It's just about got me buffaloed. I suppose one of us will be on the slate next. This is some night so far. I never saw—"

Bang! Bang! Bang!

The sound of a revolver exploding came from somewhere upstairs in the hotel.

King whirled. Raced for the main lobby. Dived down a few steps. Hit the lower floor running. Then, while everyone stood frozen to the floor, King plowed through them and was racing up the stairs three steps at a time.

The Key was behind him. The Bishop and Shakespeare were making poorer time. King darted to Ogden's door and pounded on it.

"Ogden! Ogden!" he cried. "Open up. Are you all right?"

There was no answer.

He pounded again and again. Still no answer. He put his shoulder to the door. It was light and flimsy. A powerful heave and the door crashed open.

King was standing in a vacant room and the window that shone on the porch roof was wide open.

He dove through it. Hit the top of the roof and slid. Even as he shot over the edge to the sidewalk below he was looking in every direction. Trying to find sense to the strange happenings.

He heard people running. Plenty of them. Too many.

Ogden was gone. He couldn't tell whether those shots had been fired by Ogden or someone else. Ogden had vanished. That's all he knew.

Baffled, he turned back to the hotel lobby. It was almost empty. They had rushed outside. And were beginning to come back now. Freeman came in, wide-eyed, his hair streaming.

"What's happened?" he gasped.

"It's Ogden," said King. "There was some shooting in his room. Ogden's gone. I don't know whether he jumped out of his window. Or whether someone abducted him."

FREEMAN PASSED his hand over his forehead. Did it twice. Three times. His eyes rolled a little. King stepped closer.

Freeman was babbling something. Something about it being too much. King caught him as he fell in a faint. Someone brought a pitcher of ice water from the kitchen and dashed it over his face.

The eyes of the headmaster opened. His hand went to his forehead. Weakly, this time. Already King was moving with Freeman in his arms. Walking toward the stairs.

He took Freeman to his room. The Bishop and Shakespeare followed him.

"I think, Mr. Freeman," he said, "you'd better go to bed. This is getting pretty hectic for all of us."

"Of course," said Freeman. "I don't—think I could—stand—much more of this. I've never heard of anything so horrible in my life."

"Can we help you undress?" asked King.

"No—thank you. I think I can make it," said Freeman.

He was taking off one shoe. King hesitated one moment. He went to the window in Freeman's room. Opened it and looked out. That window opened into space. The back wall of the hotel went straight down below it for a full story.

King closed the window once more.

"I think you'll be all right in this room, Mr. Freeman. If you lock your door."

"Yes, thank you," said Freeman.

He seemed confused. The Bishop and Shakespeare went out. King closed the door softly.

"Better lock it, Freeman," King called back.

"Yes, of course," said Freeman. "I will."

King heard the bolt slide. Tested the door.

"It's okay," he said. "It's locked."

Confusion again. Everyone talked. The place was in an uproar. The deputy sheriff seemed to feel that he was in charge. But he was at more of a loss to know what to do even than anyone else.

Others came in. King blinked and stared at some gaudy blouses on dark, swarthy men with jet-black hair. Patterns of lavender, pink, red, blue and green. Men that were bare-footed.

They came in silently. Stood along the side of the lobby. Staring.

King moved closer to them. Found himself standing next to a native of the town. He pointed to them.

"What the deuce are those fellows? Indians?"

"Yes," said the native. "Seminoles. Haven't you ever seen Seminoles?"

"I'm sorry. I don't believe I have ever had the pleasure before."

"They live in the Everglades."

"So I understand," said King.

King walked over to the Indian. "How long ago did you come up here?" he asked.

One, a good-looking buck with a fine physique, answered.

"We just come."

"Did you see anyone running with a man over his shoulder?"

The Seminole shook his head.

"No," he said.

"Where did you come from?" King asked.

"Up creek in dugout," said the Seminole. "Hear man killed. We come to see."

The Doctor appeared beside King as he turned away from the Indian.

"Well," he said, "it looks as though the Hernandos are in for a time of it against the golden alligator."

King turned again. Saw the young Indian looking straight at him with his black eyes. He turned and said something in Seminole to the others and they laughed.

"What are you laughing at?" King demanded.

Good-naturedly, the Indian told him.

"Hear your friend talk about gold alligator. We hunt alligator. No gold alligator. Good joke."

"Maybe you think so," said King. "But I don't."

He half turned.

A shout from the direction of the stairs that led to the second floor came to him.

*Thump! Thump! Thump!*

Someone was running down the stairs into the lobby. King pushed through the crowd. Then a huge black form leaped out of the opening in the stairs.

King crouched to tackle. It was a huge black man as large or larger than Luga. He recognized him instantly.

The same man who had taken King out of the jail. The same black man who had been swallowed by the golden alligator. Or enough like him to be his twin.

And over his shoulder he carried the struggling Professor Clinton J. Freeman!

# CHAPTER 15
## ALLIGATOR TOLL

THE FOOT of the great black man came up in a savage kick. King ducked, but not enough, although he escaped getting kicked in the face, the foot struck his shoulder, hurled him back into the crowd.

The black abductor plowed through, kicking men right and left. Plunging through the open door, he was gone into the night.

King leaped up to follow. The mob inside the hotel lobby was surging out. King tried to push through. At last he was outdoors.

"Where is he? Which way has he gone?" he yelled.

Some pointed to the right. Others to the left. No one seemed to know in the confusion which direction the black had taken.

"A flashlight! Has anybody got a flashlight?" asked King.

"Here. I've got one," someone said, and poked it into his hand. King made a wild guess, turned to the right. Then he was running out the road that led along the canal.

He flung the light beam ahead of him. Once he thought he could see a great bobbing shape far ahead of him along the bank of the canal. Then he heard the gentle drone of a powerful engine getting into motion.

He raced on. The noise of the engine increased. He recognized it instantly. It was the throbbing of the motors that propelled the fast express cruiser. The one that had left the end of the wharf in the East River. Or, at least, he decided, they were motors just like them.

Then it vanished. King turned back.

213

When he reached the town he went straight to the Hernando bungalow. Luga let him in. He found John Hernando white-faced and anxious.

"What has happened?" he asked.

King told him briefly. Then he added, "But I don't think there's anything for you and your daughter to worry about now. Not tonight. That express cruiser is gone. I heard it going down the canal.

"I'd follow it with a plane, but I haven't any flares. It would be useless, besides being practically suicide, to fly without any lights out there among those ten thousand islands." He turned to Luga. "Remember," he said, "I'm holding you responsible for the safety of Mr. Hernando and his daughter."

Inez Hernando came a little nearer. "I don't know how we can ever thank you, father and I—"

King smiled.

"You have, already," he said. He went back to the hotel. For a long time the Secret 6 met in King's room. Talked. Got nowhere. Then they went to bed.

When they came down for breakfast next morning, they found Hernando and his daughter, under the guard of Luga, waiting for them in the lobby.

"As soon as you have time," Hernando said, "I'd like to talk to you over at the house."

"Of course," said King. "We'll be right over after breakfast if there's no hurry."

"There isn't."

An hour later they were seated about the living room of the little bungalow.

"I've been thinking things over all night," said Hernando. "I couldn't sleep. I'm going to make you gentlemen a proposition. I'm sure that you've saved our lives. That is, of course, worth more than all the money in the world.

"From now on I want you gentlemen of the Secret 6 to know that Inez and I consider you as equal owners in the buried treasure. If we are successful in raising it. When the treasure is brought to the surface, we will share it equally. Split it eight ways."

He took a long breath. Then before King could say anything, he went on.

"With that in mind, since we are to share it alike, I'm going to take you out this morning and show you where the treasure is buried. I feel that the responsibility is too heavy for me. As the only man in the world that knows where it is. Sometimes I've felt that I would go insane, knowing this alone.

"Now I'm going to share it. Will you go with me in our cruiser?"

King felt the Key nudge him. "Go on," the other whispered. "Don't be a da—darned fool."

King nodded. "Of course we'll go with you. We of the Secret 6 are at the command of you and your daughter, Mr. Hernando."

"Very well, then," said the father. "Let's go."

They walked to the canal dock. Climbed into the cruiser, the *Owassa*. The engine was started. They churned out around the tail of the low-winged cabin plane and on toward the Ten Thousand Islands.

The morning was bright and clear. A typical morning of the tropics. The sun's rays were heating the air to a comfortable temperature. They threaded their way in and out of the islands. Islands of all sizes and shapes.

And as Inez steered, Hernando took a yellow gold plate from his pocket. On it was a small golden alligator and under it were capital letters and figures engraved in the gold plate.

"As we go on," he said, "I'll explain the key to the treasure. It's quite simple when you know it, but it's taken two generations to figure it out."

He pointed to the gold alligator. "You see," he said, "a very tiny x worked in the design of the rough back." He pointed to it with a stubby little finger. "It marks this point right here behind the right front leg of the alligator. Just about in the web where it joins the body."

He smiled sadly.

"As the old saying goes, 'x marks the spot.' That is the spot where the gold is buried."

KING LOOKED puzzled and shook his head.

"I'm afraid I don't quite understand," he said.

"Of course not," said Hernando. "But let me explain the inscription below. We have here XM, which are the Roman numerals for 10,000. Meaning, therefore, the Ten Thousand Islands. We have following that, 5E10NLT."

King shook his head.

"That certainly is a confusing conglomeration of signs. What do they mean?"

"I've proven to myself," Hernando went on, "that it means the treasure is buried in the Ten Thousand Islands. And in these Ten Thousand Islands, there is one island which is shaped somewhat like an alligator. The x on the gold alligator marks the spot where the gold is buried in the sands and mud off the shore.

"The 5E and the 10N gives the exact point from shore where this gold is buried."

"You mean then," King said, "in the little bay that is formed just back of the right front foot in the Island?"

"That's right," said Hernando.

"Then what does the LT stand for?"

"That took us the longest of anything to figure out," said Hernando. "But it means 'Low Tide.' Plain enough when you understand it."

"That is simple, isn't it?" said King.

"You see, we go to this island that is shaped like an alligator. The strange part of it is, that it is not marked on any map as an alligator."

"I imagine an aerial survey would show it up, wouldn't it?" asked King.

"No doubt," said Hernando. "Well, we start at low tide in the little bay that is marked x. We measure five feet out from shore toward the east. And that's from the body of the alligator island. Then we measure ten feet north from the small peninsula that forms the right leg of the alligator.

King crouched to tackle
the huge black man.

"And where those points meet you can feel the top of a huge iron chest below the mud."

"You mean," King demanded, "that all of this gold is buried in one chest?"

"I'm sure of it," said Hernando. "I haven't been able to find any other. That is why it will take huge derricks or structural works to lift that huge chest out of the mud."

"But how under the sun could they bury it?" asked King.

"Probably," said Hernando, "no one knows that today. However, it could be done quite easily with the aid of water pumps to flush out the sand and settle it.

"They could lower the chest into one of the smaller boats. There must be tons and tons of gold there. Probably the boat just managed to stay above the water with that weight on it.

"When they reached the point where it was to be buried, it was only necessary to tip over the boat.

"Then through the aid of pumps they forced water through pipes into the sand below the chest. And in that way let it settle as deep as they wished."

"By George! That's clever!" said the Doctor.

"Captain Kidd was clever," smiled Hernando.

Every man in the Secret 6 was armed with a revolver. An automatic, now. King had seen to that before they left that morning. His hands strayed near his in his pocket as they wound in and out among those islands.

For more than an hour the cruiser throbbed along. Hernando took the wheel now. They went on.

At last he pointed ahead. Pointed to a wedge-shaped peninsula. It was small. The wedge, itself, was little more than a hundred feet long. Then it branched out longer on each side.

"There," said Hernando, "is the tail of the alligator."

"Holy gee!" cried the Key. "You really mean we're getting close to where this gold is buried?"

"We're getting very close," said Hernando. "I'll show you in less than three minutes' time."

He pointed to the other islands as they passed. "You notice how close these other islands are to this one?" he asked. "It's a perfect place to hide anything of this kind. Right in the midst of this maze of islands."

King glanced around sharply. Studied the islands about them. He was frowning. Then he felt Hernando's eyes upon him.

"Anything wrong?" Hernando asked anxiously.

"I'm not sure," said King. "I guess it's just a hunch. I have the feeling that we're being watched."

"But could we be watched without seeing the person who is watching us?" asked Inez.

"I don't know. It's just a feeling. Sort of a hunch. Don't know that it amounts to anything."

"This is deeper water over here," Hernando said, going to the right of the tail. "It's like a channel down here between the islands. And this—" he pointed to a stubby little peninsula on the left—"this is the right hind leg of the island alligator."

He pointed ahead perhaps another hundred feet. "And there you see the right front leg. See it sticking out? I've never flown in a plane, but I imagine that from the air this island looks almost like a giant alligator."

He was pulling into the shore now. Had throttled the motor. The cruiser was drifting under its own momentum. He beached it before he came to the little bay that was formed in the pocket behind the right front leg.

Inez was on the shore first. King followed her. Then the rest swarmed over the bow to the shore.

"Now," Hernando said, "I'll show you. The tide is going out and in another few minutes we ought to be able to wade out and feel the top of the chest."

The Key was staring fixedly at the point in the bay where the directions that Hernando had mentioned would mean that the chest with the enormous fortune was buried. Suddenly he struck out swimming. Swimming toward the point.

King called to him.

"Hey! Come back here. What's the idea?"

THE KEY didn't answer. He kept on a few more strokes. Then reached the approximate point. Stood up. And now they could see he had been half-wading, half-swimming all the way. For the water was shallow out there.

"Is this about it, Hernando?" he asked.

Hernando nodded.

221

"Yes. Right around there somewhere. I'll have to measure it to make sure."

"Boy!" chirped the Key. "What a financial position I'm in. Over a hundred million dollars!"

"Don't be a fool," King barked. "Come on in here and follow directions."

The Key shrugged.

"Okay," he said as he waded ashore. "You ain't got any respect for a good joke."

"I've got a lot of respect for someone who might be listening that isn't supposed to be here."

"You don't see anyone?" Hernando asked.

"No, but I can't see any sense in taking a chance of telling some fishing boat nearby what we're doing."

"There aren't any fishing boats out yet," said Hernando. "I looked at the docks. All the cruisers are still in there."

"Just the same," King insisted, "I don't want to raise too much fuss around here. No telling who might be out. And I have a very strong hunch, still, that we're being watched."

Hernando looked serious.

"I'm afraid," he said, "the incidents of yesterday and last night have knocked our nerves off. But I'm going to see this thing through this morning. I'm going to show you men the chest."

He was taking off his shoes. Rolling up his trousers. He reached a point in the body part of the island.

"The tide's almost out. We'll allow six feet now, instead of five, for the center of the chest. And that'll be east. Let's see.

I'm walking facing the sun. One. Two paces," he counted. His trousers were wet. The water was up above his waist.

"Now let's see if I can find it," he said. "I'll walk from here back to the shore which forms the right leg. It'll take a little more than three paces to make the ten feet."

He waded slowly to the shore and then back again. He bent down and extended his arm at full length.

"No," he said, "I can't reach bottom yet. The tide'll have to go out a little bit more. Wait. I'll try it this way. I think I have it marked. I can feel something with my bare feet."

He bent double now. Held his nose as his head went under water. He was groping far down with his right hand. He came up for breath.

"I touched it!" he said. "I'll try once more. I always like to feel those cross-brace straps on the top of the chest to make sure I have it."

He held his nose and ducked once more.

King had been watching him the first time. Every other eye was upon him this second time except the keen eyes of King. King's eyes had been drawn out into the clear water beyond where Hernando was groping in the muddy bottom.

Suddenly he shouted a warning.

"Look! The gold alligator!"

He could see it coming through the water with hardly a move. The back of the monster was perhaps two feet below the surface now. It looked as though it were crawling up the shore.

Luga and King leaped into the water at the same time. Inez plunged in beside King. King turned and half-carried her back to the shore. He heard a frantic cry. The alligator had risen to the top of the water. It had John Hernando by the legs!

The great throat was gulping. The jaws opened. The snout of the golden monster had swallowed Hernando up to the hips.

Hernando was crying for help. Holding out his hands, trying to grasp something.

Luga was trying to pull him out. It was useless. The giant black man leaped around to the side of the 'gator. He was trying to get his thumbs in the eyes of the beast.

Hernando, in another monstrous gulp of the alligator, was sucked up between the jaws to his shoulders. Inez was fighting like a tigress to get away from King who was holding her on the shore.

But King knew there was nothing she could do. Every other member of the Secret 6 had his gun out. Was firing shot after shot at the back of the beast. King whipped out his automatic and fired also. Shouted to Luga to get out of the way.

The monster gulped once more. John Hernando disappeared down the huge throat. The jaws snapped shut. The giant alligator slipped back into water and was gone.

## CHAPTER 16
## THE GOLDEN DOOM

ALL OF the rest of that day the *Owassa* plowed the waters between the islands, searching for a sign of that golden alligator. King and the others of the Secret 6 formed a row on each side of the cruiser.

Inez, grim and white and tight-lipped, was at the wheel. No one of the party knew the waters like she. She had insisted upon going on.

Evening came. The sun was setting. King went to the girl at the wheel. She was worn. Looked as though she were about ready to drop.

"I think," King said gently, uttering the first words that had been spoken in hours, "that we'd better go back."

She stared at him wildly. Shook her head.

"No," she said. "I'll never go back until I find that 'gator."

"But we can't see," King argued. "And I don't think now there's a chance of finding the beast."

She stared at him again. Shook her head.

"No," she said.

Then she fell in a faint and King caught her in his arms. The Bishop took the wheel while King tried to revive the girl. They were moving on back.

It was almost dark when she opened her eyes. She looked up at King. And he smiled down at her.

"I think," he said, "if we can find the place where that 'gator went we'll find your father. I don't want to hold out any undue hope, but it might be possible that he's alive."

She made a brave attempt to smile. But without success.

"When you say that," she said, "I feel as though that's exactly as it's going to happen."

Then she bit her lip. Closed her eyes and King saw her fists clench to help keep back the tears. The girl opened her eyes again a short time later.

"Who's piloting?" she asked.

"The Bishop," said King. "He knows boats better than any of the rest of us. Can you tell him how to get back to the canal?"

She glanced about in the twilight.

"Tell him to look ahead for the light at the entrance of the canal," she said. "It's easier to find at night than it is in the daytime, if you don't know just where to look."

Then they were churning up the canal into Everglades City. King took her arm to steady her as they walked to her home. They turned in at the bungalow with the rest trailing a short distance behind.

Suddenly King stopped and pulled the girl to one side. He was staring at a strange figure sitting on the steps of the porch. It was dark now and he couldn't make out the man very clearly. He wasn't a white man. He was sure of that.

The man got up and came to them noiselessly. He was a Seminole. King recognized him when he spoke and was standing before them. He was the young buck he had talked to in the hotel lobby.

Inez seemed to know him too.

"Oh. Joe," she said. Then she half-turned to King. "This is Joe Buck. A friend of ours. He's worked for father sometimes. What is it, Joe? Did you want to see me?"

The Indian nodded.

"Where is your father?" he asked.

Inez bit her lip. "Father—" she gasped. Then she couldn't go on.

"Mr. Hernando isn't here now," said King, continuing. "Was there something you wanted to see him about?"

The Indian nodded.

"Maybe I talk to you," he said. "See you hotel last night. Remember you say about gold alligator and we laugh? We see gold alligator this evening."

"You saw him?" cried King.

The Indian nodded.

"Joe," Inez sobbed, "you're telling me the truth? Where? Where did you see the golden alligator this afternoon?"

"On island," said Joe. "You come. I show you. Some men have fast boat hidden under trees. Brother and I, we fish from dugout. We see gold alligator on shore.

"Then men shoot at us. We make believe fall over boat. Dead. We swim under water. Push dugout out of sight. Then get in and come here."

"You think they're there yet?" King demanded.

"Yes," nodded the Indian.

"What island was it?" demanded Inez.

"You know island," said the Indian. "Island out side on Gulf. You know island where old shell house? That the island."

"Why," she said. The girl wiped her eyes, looked up sharply. "I never thought of that. Whoever is behind all this trouble must be making their headquarters there. I know people have said they thought pirates or criminals must have built the little one-room place on the island. I've seen it once. I know where it is. It's made of coquina rock and it's hidden by a jungle."

King whirled to the giant black beside him.

"Luga," he said. "You take Miss Hernando back to the cruiser. I'm going to buy this town out of flashlights and we may need plenty of rounds of ammunition too. Hurry now. I'll meet you all at the cruiser."

It was less than ten minutes when King appeared on the dock and leaped to the after deck of the cruiser. The engine was throbbing. Inez was at the wheel. A searchlight was playing from the bow.

228

"We'll have to go slowly," she said. "I'm not too sure of the waters over there. And we can't see depth with this searchlight." They made good time going out of the canal. Then slowed as

The jungle was reverberating with the roar of guns.

they began to work their way through the island. The pulse of every man was running high.

King was standing next to Inez at the wheel. Now and then as she turned he could feel her trembling.

"I think," King said, to steady her, "everything is going to be all right."

She looked up at him in the darkness.

"I'm sure it will be if you say so."

They plowed on into the night.

About ten o'clock they ran aground. It was after midnight before they pushed the craft free again.

Went on and on.

"Don't you think," King suggested to the girl, "that you had better let the Bishop take the wheel for awhile? You ought to get some sleep."

"No, thank you," she said. "I'd rather be here. I wouldn't be able to sleep, anyway."

King nodded understandingly. "Okay," he said, "I guess you're right."

It was a little past four in the morning when the Seminole, who was perched on the very bow of the cruiser, slithered back over the forward deck.

He said, "We stop now. We in pretty shallow water. I push with pole. We not make any sound. You shut off motor."

"Are we near there?" King asked.

The Indian nodded. "Yes," he said. "About half mile. We not have lights. No sound. We come up on this side of island."

Without so much as the sound of a ripple of water the Seminole stood in the stern. Took the long pole and begun shoving the craft. Gently, silently, through the still clear water.

Inez still steered at the wheel. They were running through darkness now. With only the stars to guide them between the dots of lands. The craft moved slower and slower.

Then the Indian whispered, "That island ahead. We run nose on shore. I get out. You follow me."

THERE WAS a very gentle scraping sound a few minutes later. The cruiser stopped forward motion. They dropped silently through the water, one by one. King felt the Seminole touch his arm.

"You take hold my hand," he said. "I lead way."

He started off, holding King's hand.

King held the girl's. The girl held Luga's. And so on, they strung out. Step by step they followed the Indian into the jungle of that island. It grew thicker and thicker. They doubled up so that they might all pass through the opening in the growth that the Seminole made as they advanced.

Suddenly someone barked.

"What's that?"

King hissed an order to his own men. "They're right ahead of us," he said. "Spread out. Turn on your flashlights. Let 'em have it!"

The jungle of that island was suddenly alight with the flashes of the Secret 6. Two. Three. Four men suddenly leaped up from the ground where they had been hidden.

*Blam! Blam! Blam!*

The guns in the hands of King's men were barking. There were cries of pain and anger ahead of them. One man fell and lay still. Another pitched headlong. Tried to get up and began yelling with fear. Two others ran, limping and reeling, toward the shore just beyond them. The Secret 6 could hear them splashing in the water as they ran to get free.

A tongue of flame spat from ahead and to the left. King swerved his light instantly. But it was slowly getting gray. He realized he'd seen that form even before his light picked it out. Daylight was coming.

His light riveted on Clinton J. Freeman, the school head!

Freeman was crouched. Eyes ablaze. An ugly automatic in his hand was spitting flame into their midst. King pushed Inez down so that she fell flat rather unceremoniously. He dropped, himself. Others went down.

King held his light high on one side of a palm tree. Used it to shield his body and rose from the other side. He swerved the beam and brought it back to the place where he had seen Freeman. Let go again and again with his automatic.

It was growing brighter rapidly.

He heard a sound behind him. And at the same instant he heard Luga cry out a warning.

"Master! Behind you!"

King whirled with a smoking gun. But Luga had leaped like a panther. Leaped at that other giant black man. King knew now he had been the aide of Freeman behind this gold alligator menace. The black was the thrower of the flying garrote.

Luga struck out with his great fists.

*Smack!*

*Crash!*

They thudded with terrific force against the face of the American negro. Then they were locked in a strong wrestling hold. Over and over they rolled in the jungle.

Their holds broke. Luga was on his feet first. As the other got up Luga sprang for him. His hands reached the throat of the American black man. There was enormous power in those hands of Luga.

A choking sound came. The other negro was fighting like mad to get those hands from his throat. But there was no stopping Luga now. Even though he had a man of his own color, larger than he was.

He bent the negro backwards. Bent him double. Gave a quick snap to the neck and the giant's body went limp. Luga whirled now.

*Crack! Crack! Crack!* came the bark of Freeman's gun from behind a palm tree. King bellowed an order.

"Come on. Let's rush him!"

Men of the Secret 6 leaped out from ambush. At that, Freeman lost his nerve. Turned and ran headlong in the coming light of day for the shore a few feet behind him.

King reached the shore in time to see him plunge in the water. He was swimming desperately for another island. A stream of blood trailed behind him.

Then suddenly Joe Buck, the Seminole, yelled.

"Look! White fins!"

Every man on the shore stared. There cutting through the water were white fins. Several of them. All swimming toward

233

Freeman. There came a scream from the school headmaster. A scream of fear and mortal anguish.

Then the water churned. He disappeared from view. The water was whipped to a white froth as the sharks fought over his body. They stood there on the shore, watching in horror, for almost a full minute. Then King turned to the Seminole.

"I thought you said you and your brother jumped overboard and swam under water. How is it that the sharks didn't get you?"

"Sharks come for blood of other men," the Indian said. "We hit other men. They run into water. They bleed. Blood draw sharks from long way off. They come when last man jump in. They eat him too."

King nodded.

"Alright," he said. "That's enough of that, I guess. Now, where's this shell shack on the island?"

"Right here," said the Seminole. "I show you."

He led the way through the jungle for perhaps fifty feet or more. Bent down, and entered a low doorway.

The place had been built of chunks of coquina rock piled one upon another, with only a door. There had been a roof once. But that was caved in now. King was first inside after the Indian.

He stared in the dim light of the door. It was still dark inside. But King could barely see two figures lying on the floor, tightly bound.

Inez had slipped past him. A cry came from her lips.

"Father!"

Then the weak voice of Hernando came in answer.

Flashlights went on again. The other man was Ogden.

234

"Say, what's going on here?" Ogden demanded in the same rough tones as always. "I'm so stiff I can hardly move."

KING BROUGHT out his knife. Was cutting the ropes that bound the two men. He told Ogden what had happened.

"Well, I'll be—" Ogden began.

"Take it easy," King cautioned. "Don't forget there's a lady present. And maybe now it's about time you tell us where you fit into the picture."

"Yeah?" said Ogden. "Well who do you think you are?"

King laughed.

"No," he said. "I asked you first. What are you? You're not a merchant."

"I hope to tell you I'm not a merchant," said Ogden. "And right now I feel like the lowest detective on the force."

King chuckled.

"That's pretty good," he said. "I had you picked for the man behind this Golden Alligator organization all the time. Well, where do you fit into this thing?"

"Oh," he said. "I came in when I first saw the ad that this greenhorn from Florida ran asking for an honest man. It sounded like some kind of a con game. So they sent me over to look into it. I followed it up down here. Kind of wanted to see this country, anyway."

"Well, you certainly saw it," said King.

"You're right. I saw it," growled Ogden. "And the quicker I can get back to Miami and get a train north the better I'll like it.

"Say," he continued, "I've been trying to place you for a long

235

time. Ever since I was in that hotel room. I've seen your face somewhere. This is a queer crowd you travel around with, too.

"Why, you ain't part of the Secret 6, are you?" he demanded.

"You're doing the guessing, Ogden."

"Well, all I got to say is," he exploded, "that if the Secret 6 has been handling this job, it's about time the police took their hats off to you. And quit wasting their time chasing you. And believe me, I'm going to tell them so when I get back to the big smoke-and-clatter."

King could hear Inez Hernando talking to her father.

"Why, we thought surely you were dead, father, when we saw that alligator swallow you," he heard her say.

"You didn't think I was dead any more than I did when I went down those jaws," said Hernando. "But that isn't an alligator at all. Not a real one.

"That's the most astounding feat of engineering I have ever heard of in my life. But I almost died of fright finding it out. That alligator is a small electric submarine controlled by radio. They have a false hole built in the express cruiser.

"The alligator goes right up inside of that. And they close the door and pump out the water."

"Do you mean," the girl asked, "that you could breathe perfectly naturally inside of that horrible thing?"

"Sure," he said. "The jaws have got little rollers with spikes in them that draw you in after the jaws grab you.

"There's a chamber in there that must feed oxygen or something.

"And to think anybody would do all that for a mess of gold.

Why, you know, I've got an awful good notion to forget all about that buried treasure. It's going to take a lot to raise that stuff, anyway."

"Oh, yeah?" cut in the Key. "Listen, mister. With a little nitro-glycerine or dynamite or whatever I can get, and a darn good drill at low tide, I'll blow that thing open for you in da— darned short order."

And that is exactly what happened before the day was over.

When the explosion went off there was a tearing of metal. Then a shower of gold coins went up. Old gold coins that were of Spanish origin.

The men, including the detective, were out above their knees in the water about the blasted treasure chest, filling their pockets. Shoveling coins into the cabin of the cruiser.

Not even a tenth of the gold coins had been removed from that chest when they turned the cruiser in late afternoon toward the canal.

The Bishop's eyes were twinkling.

"You know," he said, "what I've been thinking. I'd like nothing better than to start back tomorrow morning as skipper of that express cruiser out there at the island. And perhaps I can find some way to get the golden alligator into that hole. If I can, I'll drop the beast off in Washington. Make the Smithsonian Institute a present of it."

"I'll go with you," volunteered the Doctor instantly.

King turned to the detective. "It would seem, Ogden," he said, "that we'll have room to take you back in our plane if you like. That is, if we can trust you to keep our secret."

"Sure, you can trust me," Ogden said. "After what you've done."

"Alright," King said. "It's a bargain. We'll start in the morning."

John Hernando looked at King, puzzled. And then at the others.

"But," he said, "I thought you gentlemen understood that you were all to have a share in this hundred million dollars worth of gold."

King laughed.

"With our pockets full of it now," he said, "and weighted down so we can hardly walk I should say we've done pretty well so far.

"And here's a little tip that I think maybe might help you. I wouldn't try to take any great quantity of gold out of there at a time. You know where it is now. And the lid is off. You can come and get all you want any time you like."

"That's the idea," said Hernando. "A lot of people would be better off if they took only what they needed from this life."

Inez Hernando was out at the docks when the plane left next morning.

She stopped King just before he climbed in.

"I can't tell you," she said, "how much father and I appreciate this."

There was a wistful look in her eyes.

"I'd hoped you would—stay down for some fishing. But you will come down sometime, won't you?"

"I'll certainly try," King promised.

King took off and circled about the alligator island. They looked down. "That certainly does look like a real monster alligator down there, doesn't it?"

The Key nodded solemnly.

"Yep," he said. "And I was just thinking. There's no fun in getting gold that way. When all you have to do is reach down in a chest that's as big as a bottomless well and pull it out. You appreciate it more when you work and struggle and fight for it."

King shot a curious glance at him.

"By George, Key!" he said. "I believe you're beginning to get the right idea."

"Huh?" said the Key.

He turned then and glanced back at the seat that the Bishop had occupied on the way down. The Bishop wasn't there now. His grin broadened.

"Hell!" he said. "You didn't think I was serious, did you?"

## POPULAR HERO PULPS  AVAILABLE NOW:

### THE SPIDER
- ❏ #1: The Spider Strikes — $13.95
- ❏ #2: The Wheel of Death — $13.95
- ❏ #3: Wings of the Black Death — $13.95
- ❏ #4: City of Flaming Shadows — $13.95
- ❏ #5: Empire of Doom! — $13.95
- ❏ #6: Citadel of Hell — $13.95
- ❏ #7: The Serpent of Destruction — $13.95
- ❏ #8: The Mad Horde — $13.95
- ❏ #9: Satan's Death Blast — $13.95
- ❏ #10: The Corpse Cargo — $13.95
- ❏ #11: Prince of the Red Looters — $13.95
- ❏ #12: Reign of the Silver Terror — $13.95
- ❏ #13: Builders of the Dark Empire — $13.95
- ❏ #14: Death's Crimson Juggernaut — $13.95
- ❏ #15: The Red Death Rain — $13.95
- ❏ #16: The City Destroyer — $13.95
- ❏ #17: The Pain Emperor — $13.95
- ❏ #18: The Flame Master — $13.95
- ❏ #19: Slaves of the Crime Master — $13.95
- ❏ #20: Reign of the Death Fiddler — $13.95
- ❏ #21: Hordes of the Red Butcher — $13.95
- ❏ #22: Dragon Lord of the Underworld — $13.95
- ❏ #23: Master of the Death-Madness — $13.95
- ❏ #24: King of the Red Killers — $13.95
- ❏ #25: Overlord of the Damned — $13.95
- ❏ #26: Death Reign of the Vampire King — $13.95
- ❏ #27: Emperor of the Yellow Death — $13.95
- ❏ #28: The Mayor of Hell — $13.95
- ❏ #29: Slaves of the Murder Syndicate — $13.95
- ❏ #30: Green Globes of Death — $13.95
- ❏ #31: The Cholera King — $13.95
- ❏ #32: Slaves of the Dragon — $13.95
- ❏ #33: Legions of Madness — $12.95
- ❏ **NEW:** #34: Laboratory of the Damned — $12.95

### THE MYSTERIOUS WU FANG
- ❏ #1: The Case of the Six Coffins — $12.95
- ❏ #2: The Case of the Scarlet Feather — $12.95
- ❏ #3: The Case of the Yellow Mask — $12.95
- ❏ #4: The Case of the Suicide Tomb — $12.95
- ❏ #5: The Case of the Green Death — $12.95
- ❏ #6: The Case of the Black Lotus — $12.95
- ❏ #7: The Case of the Hidden Scourge — $12.95

### G-8 AND HIS BATTLE ACES
- ❏ #1: The Bat Staffel — $13.95

### CAPTAIN SATAN
- ❏ #1: The Mask of the Damned — $13.95
- ❏ #2: Parole for the Dead — $13.95
- ❏ #3: The Dead Man Express — $13.95
- ❏ #4: A Ghost Rides the Dawn — $13.95
- ❏ #5: The Ambassador From Hell — $13.95

### DR. YEN SIN
- ❏ #1: Mystery of the Dragon's Shadow — $12.95
- ❏ #2: Mystery of the Golden Skull — $12.95
- ❏ #3: Mystery of the Singing Mummies — $12.95

## POPULAR HERO PULPS  AVAILABLE NOW:

**THE SECRET 6**
- ❏ 1: The Red Shadow $13.95
- ❏ #2: House of Walking Corpses $13.95
- ❏ #3: The Monster Murders $13.95
- ❏ *NEW:* #4: The Golden Alligator $13.95

**CAPTAIN ZERO**
- ❏ #1: City of Deadly Sleep $13.95
- ❏ #2: The Mark of Zero! $13.95
- ❏ #3: The Golden Murder Syndicate $13.95

**OPERATOR 5**
- ❏ #1: The Masked Invasion $13.95
- ❏ #2: The Invisible Empire $13.95
- ❏ #3: The Yellow Scourge $13.95
- ❏ #4: The Melting Death $13.95
- ❏ #5: Cavern of the Damned $13.95
- ❏ #6: Master of Broken Men $13.95
- ❏ #7: Invasion of the Dark Legions $13.95
- ❏ #8: The Green Death Mists $13.95
- ❏ #9: Legions of Starvation $13.95
- ❏ #10: The Red Invader $13.95
- ❏ #11: The League of War-Monsters $13.95
- ❏ #12: The Army of the Dead $13.95
- ❏ #13: March of the Flame Marauders $13.95
- ❏ #14: Blood Reign of the Dictator $13.95
- ❏ #15: Invasion of the Yellow Warlords $13.95
- ❏ #16: Legions of the Death Master $13.95
- ❏ #17: Hosts of the Flaming Death $13.95
- ❏ #18: Invasion of the Crimson Death Cult $13.95

**DUSTY AYRES AND HIS BATTLE BIRDS**
- ❏ #1: Black Lightning! $13.95
- ❏ #2: Crimson Doom $13.95
- ❏ #3: The Purple Tornado $13.95
- ❏ #4: The Screaming Eye $13.95
- ❏ #5: The Green Thunderbolt $13.95
- ❏ #6: The Red Destroyer $13.95
- ❏ #7: The White Death $13.95
- ❏ #8: The Black Avenger $13.95
- ❏ #9: The Silver Typhoon $13.95
- ❏ #10: The Troposphere F-S $13.95
- ❏ #11: The Blue Cyclone $13.95
- ❏ #12: The Tesla Raiders $13.95

**MAVERICKS**
- ❏ #1: Five Against the Law $12.95
- ❏ #2: Mesquite Manhunters $12.95
- ❏ #3: Bait for the Lobo Pack $12.95
- ❏ #4: Doc Grimson's Outlaw Posse $12.95
- ❏ #5: Charlie Parr's Gunsmoke Cure $12.95